To the *First Sisters of Oz* Immersion Class
held in Melbourne 2015—Dorothy Adamek,
Natasha Daraio, Wendy Leslie, Nas Dean and
Kristin Meacham. And of course the amazing
Margie Lawson, who taught us all so much.
It was such a privilege to spend a week
with such talented writers.  xxxxxx

# CHAPTER ONE

'I AM *NOT* serving that man on table nine,' Kat Winwood said to her co-worker Meg on her way through to the café kitchen. Aspiring actor she might be, but being polite to that Savile Row–suited, silver-tongued smart ass was way outside Kat's repertoire. She couldn't afford to lose *this* job—not unless she got the dream part in the London stage play. The role that would launch her career so she would never have to wait on another table or do another crappy—no pun intended—toilet-paper advertisement.

Meg glanced at the man before looking back at Kat. 'Isn't that Flynn Carlyon? The hotshot celebrity lawyer to those famous theatre actors Richard and Elisabetta Ravensdale?'

'Yes.' Kat gritted her teeth and unloaded the tray, stabbing the knives into the dishwasher basket as if it were Flynn Carlyon's eye sockets. How had he tracked her down? Again?

Kat didn't want her co-workers or her new boss to know she was Richard Ravensdale's scandalous secret. The secret child of his two-night-stand hotel barmaid.

*His love child.*

*Ack.* Thinking about the tacky words was bad enough. Seeing them splashed all over every London tabloid for the last three months had been nothing short of excruciating. Toenails-torn-off-with-pliers excruciating. What had love had to do with her conception? She was the product of lust. The dirty little secret Richard had paid to be removed. Obliterated.

So far no one at work had recognised her. So far. She had styled her hair differently so she didn't look like the photos that had been circulated. She had even modified her name so the press would leave her alone. For the last couple of months Flynn had been doing his level best as Richard's lawyer to get her to play happy families, but she wasn't going to fling her arms around her biological father and say 'I'm so glad

I found you' any time soon. Not in this millennium. Or the next. If Flynn thought he could wave big, fat cheques in front of her nose, or wear her down by turning up at her workplaces, then he had better think again.

Meg was looking at Kat with eyes as wide as the plates on the counter. 'Do you know him? Personally, I mean?'

'I know enough about him to know he drinks a double-shot espresso with a glass of water—no ice—on the side,' Kat said.

Meg's eyebrows lifted. 'You sure you don't want to…?'

'No.' Kat slammed the dishwasher shut. 'Absolutely not. You take him.'

Meg walked somewhat timidly towards Flynn's table where he was sitting alone with one of the daily broadsheets spread out in front of him. They exchanged a few words and Meg came back with brightly flushed cheeks and a wincing don't-shoot-me-I'm-the-messenger look. 'He said, if you don't serve him in the next two minutes he's going to speak to the manager.'

Kat glanced at her boss, Joe, who was behind

the hissing, steaming and spluttering coffee machine working his way through a list of early morning orders. If this job went kaput, she wondered how long she could couch surf in order to get enough money together to get a place of her own. At least she had the house-sitting job in Notting Hill starting this evening. The money was good, but it was only for the next four weeks. Come the first of February, she would be homeless, unless she could find another dirt-cheap bedsit. Preferably without fleas. Or bedbugs.

Any wildlife.

Kat sucked in a steadying breath, aligned her shoulders and walked to table nine with her best be-polite-to-the-annoying-customer smile stitched in place. 'How may I help you?'

Flynn's molasses-black gaze surveyed her tightly set features and lowered to the name badge pinned above her right breast. 'Kathy is it, now?' His smile was slow. Slow and deliberate. Amusement laced with mockery and a garnish of 'got you.'

Kat tried to ignore the faint prickle in her

breast where his gaze had rested. 'Would you like the usual, *sir*?'

His eyes gleamed. 'In a cup, preferably. It doesn't taste quite the same when it's poured in my lap.'

He was baiting her. Goading her. She. Would. Not. Bite. 'Would you like anything with your coffee?' she asked. 'Croissant? Muffin? Sour dough toast? Eggs? Bacon? No, perhaps not bacon. We can't have you being a cannibal, can we?'

*Damn it.*

*She'd bitten.*

The corner of his mouth tilted in a smug smile, making him look like he thought he'd won that round. 'What time do you finish work?'

Kat gave him a brace-yourself-for-round-two look. 'I'm here to serve you coffee or a meal or a snack. I'm not here to give you details about my private life.'

Flynn glanced towards the coffee machine. 'Does your boss know your true identity?'

'No, and I'd like to keep it that way.' Kat gripped her pen to stop herself from holding it to his throat to make him promise not to tell. 'Now, if you'll just give me your order…'

'Richard's agent has organised a Sixty Years in Showbiz celebration for him later this month,' he said. 'It's going to be a *This Is Your Life* format. I want you there.'

His tone suggested he was used to getting what he wanted. Every. Single. Time.

But Kat hadn't been cast in her kindergarten nativity play as a donkey for nothing. The most intractable mule had nothing on her. 'Why would I want to go to some ghastly, alcohol-soaked bragging fest about his theatre career when he *paid* my mother to get rid of me before I was born?'

Just like he'd tried to pay Kat to keep away once the news had first broken of her existence. Where had her father been when she'd needed a father? How many times during her childhood had she prayed for a dad? Someone to provide for her. Someone to protect her. Someone to love her.

Someone.

Richard hadn't even had the decency to come to see her face-to-face, but had sent his arrogant, up-himself lawyer Flynn Carlyon.

'You're being unnecessarily stubborn,' Flynn said.

*Unnecessarily?* Of course it was necessary. Her

pride was necessary. It was all she had now her mother was dead. Kat leaned down so the customers at the nearby tables couldn't hear. 'Read my lips. N. O. No.'

His hooded gaze went to her mouth, his face so close to hers she could smell his aftershave, a citrus blend with an undertone of something else, something that reminded her of a cool, dark pine forest where secrets lurked in the shifting shadows. He had recently shaved but she could see every tiny dot of stubble along his lean jaw and around his nose and mouth, the signal of potent male hormones surging through his blood.

His eyes dipped to the open V of her shirt. Only the top two buttons were undone, revealing little more than the base of her neck, but the heat in his gaze made her feel as if she was standing there bare breasted. She straightened as if someone had fisted the back of her shirt and pulled her upright.

*Do. Not. Look. At. His. Mouth*. Kat chanted it mentally while her eyes continued their traitorous feasting on the contours of his lips. He was smiling again as if he knew exactly the effect he had on her. How could a man she hated so much have such a gorgeous mouth? He had the sort of mouth you could only describe as sinful. Smoking-hot, sex-up-against-the-kitchen-bench sinful. Sex-with-the-curtains-wide-open sinful. The upper lip was straight across the top, but the lower lip more than made up for it. It was full, sensual. The midpoint in perfect alignment with the sexy shallow cleft in his chin.

The only reason she was obsessing about his mouth was because she was doing 'Winter Deep Freeze' with her best friend, Maddie Evans. Their celibacy pact had started in November and, with only a month to go, Kat was determined to win. She had to prove a point, not just to her best friend, but also to herself. No way was she going to play out the script of her mother's life. Bad date after bad date. Sex that scratched an itch but left filthy finger marks on the fabric of her soul.

Who said Kat couldn't go three months without sex?

She *could*. And she damn well *would*.

One of the customers tried to move past, bumping against Kat so she had to suck in her stomach and press herself against Flynn's table. The brush of his trouser leg on her knee sent a lightning zap of heat through her body. Hot. Searing. Scorching. So scorching she expected to look down and see a singed and smoking hole in her thick black tights.

She stepped back once the customer had gone, pen poised pointedly. 'Espresso? Water no ice?'

'He's your only living parent,' Flynn said.

Kat sent him a look that would have frozen mercury. 'So? With relatives like him, lead me to the nearest orphanage. I'm checking in.'

Something moved in his gaze as quickly as a camera-shutter click. But then his lazily slanted smile came back. 'Are you going to get my coffee?'

'Are you going to take no for an answer?'

His eyes beneath those dark, winged brows roved her lips. Did he feel the same flicker of animal attraction deep and low in his belly? Kat could feel it now. The pulse of lust thrumming in her blood every time his dark eyes trapped hers, as if he too were thinking of what it would feel like to have her stripped naked and pinned beneath his body.

Or against the kitchen bench.

*Be still her heart, her pulse, her giddy-with-excitement girly bits.*

Another customer came past, but this time Kat turned so her back was to Flynn. *Big mistake.* She could sense his gaze on her bottom, burning through the layer of her boring black uniform to the satin and lace secrets beneath. She turned and carefully masked her features, but even so she could feel the warmth glowing in her cheeks.

'What are you doing for dinner this evening?'

Kat put her hands on her hips, anchoring her resolve in case it took it upon itself to quit its shift. 'I suppose this is a rarity for you? A woman actually having the willpower to say no to you?'

The glint in his eye made something in her stomach swoop. 'Nothing I like more than a challenge. The harder, the better.'

Joe came up carrying a tray of coffees. 'Kathy, are you working the floor or flirting with the customers?'

'Sorry, Mr Peruzzi,' Kat said. 'This customer has a…a complicated order.'

'Tables seven and ten are waiting for their bills,'

Joe said. 'And tables two and eight need clearing and resetting. I'm running a café, not a freaking dating agency.'

Kat smiled sweetly even though her back teeth were glued together. 'There isn't a man inside this café I would be even *remotely* tempted to date.'

Joe hustled past and Flynn said, 'Would you be remotely tempted to serve them some coffee?'

She held his mocking look with steely intent. 'You won't win this, Mr Carlyon. I don't care how many jobs you make me lose. I will not be told what to do.'

He leaned back in his chair as if he had all the time in this world and the next. 'By the way, you were great in that toilet-paper ad,' he said. 'Very convincing.'

Kat could feel her back molars grinding down to her mandible. At this rate, her dental hygienist would be charging a search fee. The only thing more humiliating than doing a job like that toilet-paper gig was having your worst enemy see it. 'So, just the coffee, or would you like a full breakfast to clog your arteries?'

He gave a low, deep chuckle that made the backs of her knees shiver. 'I'll have some cake.'

Kat frowned. It was seven thirty in the morning. Who ate cake at that hour? *'Cake?'*

'Yep.' He winked at her. 'And I'm going to eat it too.'


'What was that all about?' Meg asked when Kat came back to the servery. 'You're so red I could cook table four's buckwheat pancakes on your cheeks.'

'I swear to God I'm going to explode if I have to go anywhere near that man,' Kat said. 'I seriously do not get what women see in him. So what if he's good looking? He's an arrogant jerk.'

'I think he's gorgeous.' Meg's expression had that whole star-struck thing going on. 'He has such dark-brown eyes you can't tell where his pupils begin and end.'

Kat got out a large slice of devil's food cake and liberally coated it with cream. 'There,' she said. 'That should fix him. If that doesn't give him a heart attack, nothing will.'

'I don't think there's anything wrong with his

heart,' Meg said. 'He looks like he seriously works out. And he's so tall. Did you see him stoop as he came in?'

'I suppose he has to be that tall to allow room for all that ego,' Kat muttered, picked up the coffee and made her way back to his table.

'Here you go.' She placed the plate, the coffee and the glass of water in front of him.

Flynn cocked an eyebrow. 'Aren't you going to give me a cake fork?'

Kat rounded her eyes in mock surprise. 'Oh, you actually *know* how to eat with cutlery, do you? I would never have guessed.'

His lopsided smile did that swoop and dive thing to her belly. 'You should be onstage.'

'Yeah, well, that's the plan.'

'So how's that going for you?'

Kat wasn't going to tell him anything about her audition in a few days' time in the West End. The AR Gurney play *Sylvia* couldn't have come along at a more opportune time. It was one of her favourite plays and she knew deep in her bones she was right for the part of the dog Sylvia. Audiences worldwide loved the notion of a human playing a dog. If she landed the role and did it well, it could launch her career. She wanted the part on her own merit, not because of whose DNA she shared. She didn't trust Flynn not to leak something to Richard Ravensdale, who might then open doors she wanted to open with her own talent.

'I'll go and get that fork for you.' She gave Flynn a tight smile. 'Or would you like a shovel?'

His eyes held hers with implacable intent. Hinting at an iron will that was energised, excited, exhilarated by the mere whiff of a challenge. 'I'd like to see you tonight.'

'Not going to happen,' Kat said. 'I have an appointment with a cat and a fur ball.'

That glint was back in his eyes. 'I didn't know you had a cat.'

'I don't,' she said. 'I've picked up a new house-sitting job. The agency I work for occasionally rang me this morning. The person they had for the post had to pull out at short notice due to a family crisis. Apparently the cat is one of those ones that are too precious to go to a boarding centre. It has—' she put her fingers into air quotes '—issues.'

'How long will you be house-sitting?'

'A month.'

'Where in London?'

Kat gave him a cynical look. 'Why would I tell you? You'd be on my doorstep day and night pestering me to meet my sperm donor.'

The corner of his mouth tipped up in an enigmatic smile. 'So, I guess I'll see you when I see you.'

*Not if I can help it.* She swung around and stalked back to the kitchen.

Flynn's gaze followed that deliciously pert behind until it disappeared into the servery. The thrill of the chase had always excited him but *this* chase was something else. Kat Winwood was hot. Flames, flares, and hissing and spitting fireworks hot.

It was amusing to set the bait and sit back and wait for her to take it. She pretended to hate him. To loathe the ground he walked on, the space he occupied. The air he breathed.

But behind the fiery flash of her green-grey gaze he could see something else. Something she was at great pains to conceal. That betraying flicker of attraction. The way her pupils flared like spilled ink. The way she swept the tip of her tongue over her lips. The way her eyes kept tracking to his mouth as if drawn there by an invisible, irresistible force.

He felt the same stirring in his body whenever he was near her. Lust rumbled and rolled through his body like a cannonball. It was taking longer than usual to get her to admit her interest. But that was what made him all the more determined. The challenge made his blood tick and flick with excitement. He was used to having anyone he wanted. Dating had become almost boring. He couldn't remember the last time a woman had said no to him.

Not since Claire had walked out on their engagement.

He ducked back out from under the crime-scene tape in his mind that blocked him from thinking of how desperate he had felt back then. Desperate to be with someone. To have a family.

To have a future to make up for the blank space of his past.

He wasn't that commitment-with-a-capital-C man now.

He was a lower-case lover. The chase, the conquest, the 'don't call me I'll call you' was how he played things now.

And he wanted to play with Kat Winwood.

He wanted to feel her sexy little body gripping him like a clamped fist. To feel her mouth breathing fire over his skin. To feel her tongue twisting, twirling and tangling with lust around his. He wanted to hear that cute little Scottish accent screaming out his name as she convulsed around him.

Kat might be playing it cool, but how long could she ignore the heat that flared between them?

Especially when he was going to be a lot closer to her than she'd bargained for.

*A whole lot closer.*

# CHAPTER TWO

*OKAY, THERE HAS to be catch.* Kat unlocked the door of the Notting Hill Victorian mansion the house-sitting agency had assigned her. Call her a pessimist, but she knew from experience that anything that looked too good to be true usually was. But so far all she could see was luxury. The sort of opulent luxury she had dreamed of since she was a kid growing up on a council estate in Glasgow. Even the air inside the house smelt rich. The grace notes of an exclusive perfume and the base note of some sort of essential oil made her nostrils quiver in sensory delight. She closed the door and the stunning crystal chandeliers overhead tinkled against the bitter early January wind, as if disturbed by the whispery breath of a ghost.

Kat ignored the faint shiver that crept over her scalp. She was being ridiculous. Of course she was. It was her nerves because of the audition next week. She could feel the moths fluttering in her belly even now. Big, winged ones, beating against the walls of her stomach like razor blades. If she got the part in the West End play and her career finally took off she would never have to waitress or house-sit again. She would be able to buy her own luxury mansion, have her own space instead of borrowing a stranger's.

Usually the houses she looked after were a little more modest than this. But she wasn't complaining. Although, four weeks of living with such decadence was going to make it hard to adjust once she went back to a poky little bedsit—if she was lucky enough to secure one.

Someone had kindly left the heating on…or maybe that was because of Monty, the cat Kat was supposed to be minding along with the house. Kat wasn't a great fan of cats. She was more of a dog person. But apparently Monty was a delicate 'inside' cat, which meant there wouldn't be any nasty unmentionable creatures to deal with because he wouldn't be out at night hunting.

Anyway, turning down a job because of a bit of a feline prejudice wasn't an option just now.

Besides, she was an actor, wasn't she? She would *pretend* to like the cat.

Kat wandered through the house looking for the cat…or so she told herself. What she was really looking at were all the photos of the couple that lived there. The Carstairses were both professionals—the wife was a GP and the husband a barrister, and they had two gorgeous kids, a boy and a girl who were both under five. They had taken the kids to Australia to see relatives—or so the agency lady had told her.

It was hard to look at those photos and not feel a little twinge of envy. Well, maybe not just a little twinge. More like a large fist grabbing at her innards and twisting them until the blood supply was cut off.

Kat's childhood hadn't looked anything like these kids' childhoods. Firstly, she hadn't had a father. She had one *now* but that was another story. Secondly, her mother hadn't looked as relaxed and content as the mother in the photos. Her mother had spent most of Kat's childhood inviting the wolf at the door in for sleepovers. And as for any exotic holidays abroad…the only 'overseas' holidays she'd had with her mother had been to visit her grandparents in the Outer Hebrides on the Isle of Harris. But typically those visits had only lasted a couple of days before her mother had got tired of the I-told-you-so lectures from her strict Presbyterian parents.

Kat found more photos in the gorgeous sitting room that overlooked the even more gorgeous garden. Even though it was back to its bare bones, being the first week in January, it would be the perfect place for a couple of kids to play on long summer afternoons, or for two adults to sit out there with a glass of chilled wine and chat about their day while they watched the children gambolling about.

Funny, but at her last damp and mouldy bedsit the rain had looked every bit as bleak and dismal as winter rain could be. It would drip down the panes of glass…on both sides, unfortunately. But at the Carstairses' house the droplets trickled down—thankfully on the outside only—the triple-glazed windows like strings of glittering diamonds.

Kat shifted her gaze to a photo in a frame on a mahogany drop-sided table next to the window. It was a Christmas photo: she could see a brightly decorated Christmas tree with heaps of beautifully wrapped presents underneath its branches. The same tree was still in situ—it was on her lists of tasks to pack it away before the family returned. There were ten or twelve people in the photo, the children in the front, the shorter adults at the sides and the tallest at the back. But there was one man who stood head and shoulders over everyone else. She picked up the photo with a hand that wasn't quite steady.

What was *he* doing there?

Kat clenched her teeth so hard she could feel the tension turning the muscles in her neck and shoulders into boulders. She put the photo down before she was tempted to smash it against the wall. She swung away from the window, pacing the carpeted floor like a swordfish in a salad bowl.

*What was Flynn Carlyon doing in the bosom of the family she was house-sitting for?*

The sticky feet of suspicion crawled up her spine and over her scalp. She had thought it a little odd that the people hadn't wanted to speak to her on the phone, especially since there was a pet involved. People were sometimes fussier over who minded their pets than their kids. But her supervisor had said another client had recommended her. Not just the agency, but her. By name.

Which client?

Kat was starting to smell a six-foot-four, Savile Row–suited rat with sooty black hair and eyes the colour of the espresso he drank.

*What was Flynn up to?*

Kat had told him in no uncertain terms she wanted nothing to do with her father.

No contact. No favours. No money.

She hadn't spoken to the press even though they had hounded her for weeks. She had gone underground to escape them. She kept a low profile when she was out and about. She wore her hair under a beanie or wore sunglasses. It might be considered a little crazy in the dead of winter, but at least she was able to avoid eye contact. She was even auditioning under a false name in order to distance herself from the Ravensdales. She couldn't win either way. If she auditioned under her real name, Katherine Winwood, everyone would know she was Richard Ravensdale's love child, so she might be given the part for all the wrong reasons. Everyone would be crying nepotism. She wanted the part because of her talent, not because of her bloodline. A bloodline she was intent on ignoring, thank you very much, because her father hadn't wanted her in the first place. Why on earth would she want to connect with the man who had not only insisted on her mother having an abortion but *had paid* her to do it?

What was it about the Ravensdales and money? Did they think they could pay her to go away one minute and then lure her back the next?

Why couldn't they accept she wanted nothing to do with them?

Kat had been tempted to meet Miranda, her half-sister. It felt a little weird to think she had half-siblings—twin brothers ten years older, Julius and Jake, and then Miranda who was only two months older than Kat. Two months. Which just showed what a jerk Richard Ravensdale was because he had still been seeing Kat's mother while he'd been reconciling with Elisabetta Albertini, his then ex-wife. His soon-to-be ex-wife again if the tabloids were to be believed.

But, in spite of her longing for a family to belong to, Kat wanted nothing to do with any of them. Not even Jasmine Connolly, the bridal designer who had grown up at Ravensdene with Miranda. Jasmine was the gardener's daughter and had recently become engaged to Jake Ravensdale. She seemed a nice, fun sort of girl, someone Kat would like to be friends with, but hanging out with anyone who had anything to do with the Ravensdales was *not on*.

Kat was used to being an only child. She was used to being without a family. She was still getting used to being without her mother. Not that they'd had the best mother and daughter relationship or anything. Kat always felt a little conflicted when it came to days like Mother's

Day. Somehow the pretty pink cards with their flowery and sentimental verses and messages didn't quite suit the relationship she had with her mother. Growing up, she'd felt unspeakably lonely because of it.

If you couldn't talk to your mother, then who could you talk to?

Kat certainly didn't need a rich and famous family to interfere with her life and her career. She was going to make it on her own. She didn't need any favours, leg-ups or red carpet invitations. And she certainly didn't need any hotshot, too-handsome-to-be-trusted London lawyers manipulating things in the background. What was his connection with the Carstairs family? Was Mr Carstairs a work colleague? What did Flynn hope to achieve by having her mind a colleague's house? Did he think it would give him a better chance of 'accidentally' bumping into her so he could flirt and banter with her?

Over her dead and rotting body it would. There was no way she wanted anything to do with Flynn Carlyon. He was exactly the sort of man she avoided. Too good-looking, too sure of himself, too much of a ladies' man.

Too tempting.

There was the sound of a miaow and Kat turned around to see a large Persian cat the colour of charcoal strutting in as if he owned the place. *Which he kind of did.* 'Hello, Monty.' She reached down to pat him. 'I believe we're going to be housemates for a few weeks.' Monty gave her a beady look from eyes as yellow as an owl's and shrank away from her outstretched hand with a hiss and a snarl that sounded scary enough to be in a horror movie. A Stephen King movie.

She straightened. 'So it's going to be like that, is it? Well, you'd better get over yourself quick smart, as I'm the one in charge of feeding you.'

The cat slunk out of the room with its tail twitching like a conductor's baton.

Kat rolled her eyes. 'That's why I prefer dogs. They're not stuck-up snobs.'

The rain was coming down in icy sheets when Kat came back from picking up some shopping an hour later. There was food for the cat and some basic things in the pantry but she preferred to purchase her own food. She would have or-dered it online but her credit card was still maxed out after her mother's funeral. The thought of that big, fat cheque Flynn Carlyon had dangled under her nose when he'd come into the café a couple of months back was dismissed by her pride.

No way was she being bought.

No. Way.

If she wanted to speak to the press, she would. If she wanted to connect with her father, she would in her own good time. Not that it was going to happen any time soon, if ever. She couldn't imagine a time when she would feel anything but disdain for a man who had used her mother so callously. Just because she shared some of his DNA didn't mean she was going to strike up a loving, all-is-forgiven father-daughter relation-ship with him. Where had he been when things had been so dire growing up? He hadn't con-tributed anything towards her upbringing. Not a brass razoo. He had paid off her mother and then had promptly forgotten about her. The money he had paid had gone before Kat was a year old. She and her mother had lived in hardscrabble poverty for most of her childhood.

The shame of not having enough, of wanting more but never having enough to pay for it, was not something she could easily forget. Her mother had worked a variety of cleaning and bar jobs, none of them lasting very long. Her mother would always have 'an issue' with someone in the workplace. Kat had felt utterly powerless as she'd watched her mother swing from manic enthusiasm for a new job to coming crashing down in a depressed stupor when she lost it and/or walked out. Her black mood would last for weeks, sometimes months, until the cycle would begin all over again.

Kat had decided as a young child she would do everything in her power to make life better for her mother. She'd thought if she could find a way to get her mum some help, to get her some financial stability and support, then her mother might magically turn into the mother she'd dreamed of having.

But in the end she hadn't been able to do it. Her mother had died of cancer, perhaps not in dirt-poor poverty, but close enough to make Kat feel nothing but anger towards her biological father who could at the very least have made their lives decent instead of desperate.

It wasn't just anger she felt. It *hurt* to think Richard Ravensdale hadn't cared anything about her. His own flesh and blood had been nothing to him. Just a problem that had to be removed and then swiped from his memory. Permanently.

The parking space outside the Carstairses' house was tight, especially with the rain obscuring her vision. Kat's car wasn't big by any means but trying to get it into the tiny space between the shiny black BMW and the silver Mercedes was like trying to squeeze an elephant's foot into a ballet slipper.

Not going to happen.

She blew out a breath and tried again. But now a line of cars coming home for the day was banking up behind her. In spite of the biting cold, beads of sweat broke out over her brow. She put her foot on the accelerator and nudged the car backwards, but someone behind her impatiently tooted their horn and put her off her game. She slammed on the brakes and gripped the steering wheel even tighter. She was tempted to roll down the window and give the driver behind the finger, but then a tall figure appeared at her driver's door.

*Oh, God.* A surge of panic seized Kat's chest. Road rage. Was she to be beaten senseless? Dragged out of the car and kicked and shoved and stomped on and then thrown to the gutter like a bit of trash? She could see the headlines: *Struggling actor beaten to a pulp over traffic incident.* She could see the social media footage. It would go viral. Millions of people would view her demise. She would finally be famous but for all the wrong reasons.

Kat turned to face her opponent with a bravado she was nowhere near feeling. This was the upside of having gone to acting classes. She could do 'affronted driver' down pat. But the man wasn't growling and swearing or shaking his fists at her. He was *smiling*.

She rolled down her window and glowered at Flynn Carlyon's amused expression. 'I would ask you what the hell you're doing here but I'm not sure I want to know the answer.'

He leaned down so his head was on a level with hers. Kat dearly wished he hadn't. This close she could see the bottomless depth of his glinting eyes. The cleanly shaven jaw of this morning was gone; in its place was the dark shadow of late-in-the-day, urgent male stubble peppered all over it. And, if that wasn't enough to make her heart come to a juddering stop, some strands of his ink-black hair fell forward over his forehead, giving him a rakish look. 'Want me to park it for you?'

'No, thank you,' Kat said, doing a prim school-mistress tone straight out of her actor's hand-book. 'I'm perfectly capable of parking my own car.' Not quite true. She had always had trouble with reverse parking, especially in busy traffic. She had failed her driving test three times be-cause of it.

His smile stretched to tilt one corner of his mouth. 'It looks like it.'

Kat clenched her teeth hard enough to crack a walnut. And to add insult to injury two more cars tooted. Flynn straightened and turned, flattening his back against the side of her door as he waved the traffic through. The fabric of his coat—one hundred per cent cashmere, if she was any judge—was close enough for her to touch. She gripped the steering wheel like her hands were stuck there with superglue and wondered why the planets had conspired against her to have Flynn Carlyon witness her humiliation in a busy Notting Hill street.

He turned back and tapped the roof of her car. 'Watch out for the car behind,' he said. 'It's mine.'

She double-blinked. 'Yours?'

'Yeah, didn't I tell you?' That annoying smile again. 'We're neighbours.'

Later, Kat didn't know how she'd parked that car without ramming into his. She wanted to. Oh, how she wanted to. Nothing would have given her more pleasure than to smash up his pride and joy. To reverse her car at full throttle time and time again.

Crash. Bang. Crash. Bang. Crash. Bang.

She got out of her car and pretended she didn't notice how out of place it looked sandwiched between his showroom-perfect BMW and the silver

Mercedes. It looked like a donkey at the starting gates at Royal Ascot.

Kat joined him on the footpath. 'Just answer me one question. Did you have something to do with my appointment at the Carstairses' next door?'

'They were looking for a house-sitter. Your name came up.'

Kat narrowed her gaze. 'Why me? You know nothing about me.'

'On the contrary, Miss Winwood,' he said with a slow smile that had a hint of imperiousness, 'I know quite a lot about you.'

'Like what?'

'Your father is Richard—'

'Apart from that.'

'Why don't you want to meet him?' Flynn said.

'The first time we spoke you wanted to *stop* me meeting him. Now you want me to come to his stupid party. How do I know what he'll want tomorrow or the next day?'

He gave a loose shrug of a very broad shoulder. *Did he row for England? Work out? Lift bulldozers in the gym?* 'He's changed his mind since then,' he said. 'He wants to make amends. He feels bad about the way things turned out.'

Kat gave a scoffing laugh. '"Turned out"? Things didn't "turn out." He was the one who tried to get rid me as a baby. He treated my mother appallingly. The only thing he feels bad about is my mother finally telling me of my origin. That's what he's upset about. He thought his dirty little secret had gone away. His agent is probably only doing this as some sort of popularity stunt. I bet Richard couldn't care less about meeting me. He just doesn't want his adoring public to see him as a deadbeat dad.'

'The rest of the family would like to meet you. They haven't done you or your mother any wrong.'

There was a part of Kat that conceded he was right, but she wasn't ready to join them for family get-togethers, because it would pander to Richard Ravensdale—not to mention Flynn, who was acting for him. 'What about his wife, Elisabetta Albertini?' she said. 'I bet she isn't waiting for me with open arms to welcome me to the bosom of the family.'

'No, but she too might change her mind when she sees how sweet and lovable you are.'

Kat shot him a withering look. 'But I thought she was going to divorce him. Who will you represent if she does? Don't you act for both of them?'

'I'm hoping it won't come to that. A divorce would be costly to both of them.'

'Why should you mind?' she said. 'Either way, you'd still get paid bags and bags of money.'

'Contrary to what you might think, money is not my primary motivation in representing my clients,' he said. 'The Ravensdales are people I admire and respect and am deeply fond of. Now, if you'll excuse me, I'd like to get in out of this rain.'

Kat had barely noticed the rain but now that he mentioned it she could feel it dripping down the back of her coat collar in icy shards. God knew what her hair looked like. She could feel it plastered to her scalp and over her shoulders like a Viking helmet. Not that she cared a fig for how she looked in front of Flynn Carlyon. She didn't care for his opinion one way or the other. So what if he only ever surrounded himself with beautiful people?

She. Did. Not. Care.

She balled her hands into fists. 'What do you possibly hope to achieve by having me installed next door?'

His look was inscrutable. 'If you're so uncomfortable with the notion then why not call the agency and be transferred?'

Kate would have done so if it hadn't been for the money. The Carstairs family was paying extra for her to Skype them each day with the cat. Weird, but true. She only hoped Monty would agree to sit on her lap long enough to look at his family on the other side of the globe. 'Once I commit to something, I don't like to let people down,' she said.

'Nor do I,' he said and, giving her another one of those annoying winks, he turned and went inside his house.

Flynn was enjoying a quiet drink in his sitting room, with his little dog Cricket snoring at his feet while he went over a client's brief, but his mind kept drifting to his conversation with Kat Winwood. *Conversation?* More like a verbal fencing match. As soon as he'd met her last October he had felt a compulsive desire to see her again. Even if Richard had told him to forget about making contact with her, Flynn knew he would still have done so, for his own reasons, not his client's.

She was simply unforgettable.

Her sparking green-grey eyes, her beautiful, wild brown hair with its copper highlights, her gorgeous figure, her razor-sharp tongue and acerbic wit were a knockout combination. A sexy, heady cocktail he wanted to get smashed on as soon as he could.

When his neighbours had phoned and asked him if he knew anyone who could house-sit for them at short notice, he had immediately thought of her. Why wouldn't he recommend her? He knew she was well respected at the agency. It suited him to have her close. He was a fully paid-up member of the keep-your-friends-close-and-your-enemies-closer club.

Not that she was really his enemy. She was a challenge he couldn't resist.

As he saw it, Kat had everything to win by making peace with her father. Not that Flynn believed Richard was trying to make up for the way he had handled things. He wasn't so gullible he couldn't see what his client's motives were. He knew it had more to do with Richard wanting everyone to think he was doing the right thing by Kat. He hadn't been a class act in how he had treated Kat's mother, but as for his apology being genuine and heartfelt? Well, Richard hadn't received all those acting awards for nothing.

Kat was being stubborn on principle. Flynn could understand it but he wanted her to put her prejudices aside and form some sort of relationship with the man whose DNA she carried. She was lucky. At least she knew who both her parents were.

He had no idea who his were. And he never would.

For the last couple of months Kat had filled his every waking moment and far too many of his sleeping ones. He wasn't sure what it was about her that intrigued him so much. He'd had his fair share of beautiful women over the years since Claire had left him, but none had made him feel this power surge of attraction. He looked forward to seeing her, to bantering with her. She was smart and funny, and her broad Scottish accent was so darn cute it never failed to make him smile. He liked her energy, the feisty flare of temper that made him wonder what she would be like in bed. All that passion had to have an outlet. He wanted to be the trigger that made her explode.

He *had* to get her to that party. It was his mission. His goal. It wasn't just because Richard had entrusted him with the task of getting her to meet with him. It was because once Flynn set his mind to a task he allowed nothing and no one to get in his way. He had faced down huge challenges all of his life and won.

This was no different.

The party was going to be televised live. His reputation would be on the line. Everyone knew he had been assigned the task of getting Kat into the bosom of the family. He couldn't accept failure. He had to pull this off no matter what. Failure wasn't in his vocabulary. His professional tag line was 'Flynn Equals Win.'

Kat was being pig-headed about meeting Richard out of loyalty to her mother. That wasn't a bad thing. He understood it. Admired it, even. But this wasn't just about her father. The whole family wanted to embrace her because they were decent people who wanted to do the right thing by her. She had no one else. He couldn't see why she wouldn't welcome the chance to be included in one of London's wealthiest and most talented families. Plus they could fast-track her to the fame she was striving for.

Cricket lifted his head off his crossed paws and gave a sharp bark.

'You want a walk at this time of night?' Flynn said.

Cricket bounced up and yapped in excitement, spinning in circles like a dervish on an upper. Flynn put his papers down and smiled. 'You do realise this is why my mother got rid of you? You're seriously high maintenance.'

Cricket ran to pick up his lead, trailing it behind him and getting his stubby little legs tangled up in it in his excitement. Flynn bent down to clip the lead on the dog's collar and ruffled his odd little one-up, one-down ears. 'Come on, you crazy little mutt. But, if it starts snowing, don't say I didn't warn you.'

# CHAPTER THREE

KAT WAS ON her way to bed when she realised she hadn't seen Monty since she had given him dinner—or tried to. He had turned up his nose at her and stalked off with his tail twitching as though someone had sent an electric current through him. The Skype attempt hadn't gone well either—she bore the scratches on her hands to prove it. But at least she had met the Carstairs family, who were as lovely as they appeared in their array of photographs. They assured her Monty would soon be purring contentedly in her lap once he established trust. They never once mentioned their handsome neighbour, which seemed a bit suspicious to Kat. If he was smack, bang in the middle of their most recent Christmas photo, then surely they would mention him in passing?

She couldn't stop looking at that photo every time she went into the sitting room. It wasn't just

Flynn's smiling face that pulled her gaze, but the way he was so comfortable around those kids. The little boy called Josh was looking up at Flynn in what looked like a state of hero worship. There was another photo in the study, with Flynn and the Carstairses' little girl Bella, who was about three years old, sitting on Flynn's knee. She was sucking her little thumb and leaning contentedly against Flynn's broad chest as he read to her from a children's picture book.

It made Kat wonder if he planned to settle down and have his own family one day. He was known to be a bit of a ladies' man but not as much of a full-on playboy as Jake Ravensdale had been before becoming engaged to Jasmine Connolly. But if Flynn had been seeing anyone on a regular basis lately there hadn't been anything in the press—or not that Kat had been able to find.

The only person he had been seen with, ironically enough, was her.

She looked through each of the rooms but Monty wasn't anywhere to be seen. There was a circular patch of sooty fur where he had been sleeping on the Carstairses' white linen bed but no sign of him in the flesh...or fur, so to speak.

She checked all the windows, even though she hadn't opened any, to make sure he hadn't escaped. But when she checked the laundry window she noticed there was a cat flap on the bottom of the door. She hadn't noticed it there before, but then, why would she? Monty was supposed to be an inside cat. Kat had cleaned his litter tray earlier. He wasn't supposed to go outside and get wet, or snowed on, or run over by a car...or bring in—*gulp*—horrible hunting trophies. The cat flap was unlocked. Should she close it? What if he was outside and couldn't get back in?

Kat decided to do another thorough search of the house before she locked the cat flap. Surely Monty wouldn't go outside on such a foul night? What was that saying about mad dogs and Englishmen? Or was that just a saying about summer?

She was coming through the sitting room when she heard the bump of the cat flap opening and closing. Then she heard the sound of Monty giving a weird-sounding miaow. Every hair on Kat's scalp fizzed at the roots. Every knob of her spine froze. She knew what *that* was. That was a victory miaow. The sort of miaow a cat makes when it lands its prey and was about to show it off to its owners.

But Kat wasn't his owner. She didn't want to see his handiwork. No way. This was why she didn't own a cat. This was why she didn't even *like* cats. They brought in stuff, horrible stuff, like dead birds and...and...she couldn't even think the word without wanting to jump on a chair and scream. Dread as cold as the snow falling outside chugged through her veins. A hedgehog climbed up her windpipe until she couldn't take a breath. Fear tightened her chest, making her heart go into arrhythmia so bad any decent cardiologist would have rushed for a defibrillator.

Her eyes were glued to the door of the sitting room. It was like a scene in a Friday night fright film. She was frozen with primal fear, unable to move a step forward or a step back. Her feet were nailed to the floor. Monty made that muffled miaow again from just outside the sitting room, the miaow that sounded like he had his mouth full of…something.

*No. No. No.* Kat chanted manically. This couldn't be happening. Not to her. Not on her first night in this lovely house. Lovely houses like this didn't have dreadful, ghastly, horrid, unmentionable creatures inside them…

It was so quiet she could hear each soft pad of Monty's paws on the carpet as he came round the door into the sitting room. *Puft. Puft. Puft. Puft.* Her eyes widened in horror when she saw what was dangling from his mouth. *'Eeeeeek!'* She screamed so loudly she was vaguely aware she might shatter the chandeliers or windows. Or wake the neighbours. In France.

But then the stupid cat let the thing go. And it wasn't dead! It streaked across the floor right next to Kat's feet and disappeared under one of the sofas.

Kat bolted from the room so fast she could have qualified for the Olympics. She snapped the door shut behind her and fled to the front door, barely stopping long enough to grab her coat from the coat stand. She didn't bother with gloves—she would never have been able to get them on her shaking hands. She had only taken one flying step out of the Carstairses' house when she came face to face with Flynn, who was walking a weird-looking dog.

He frowned and steadied her with a hand on her arm. 'Are you all right? I heard you screaming and—'

Kat pointed back at the house with a quaking finger. 'In—in there… M-Monty brought in a…a…'

'A what?'

'I can't say it,' she said. 'Please will you get rid of it for me? *Please?* I'll never be able to sleep knowing it's in there.'

'What's in there?'

Kat absolutely never cried. Not unless it was written in the script. Then she could do it, no problem. But fear colliding with relief that someone had come to her rescue made her want to throw herself on Flynn's chest and howl like a febrile teething baby. She bit her bottom lip, sure she was going to bite right through before she could stop it trembling. 'I—I have this thing...a phobia...I know it's silly but I—I just can't help it.'

He put his gloved hand on her shoulder. Even though there were layers of fabric between his skin and hers, she felt something warm and electric go right through her body from the top of her shoulder to the balls of her feet. 'Did Monty bring in a mouse?'

Kat squeezed her eyes shut and put her hands over her ears. 'Don't say that word!'

His hand slipped down from her shoulder to take her bare hands in his gloved ones. 'Look at me, Kat.'

Kat looked. But he wasn't laughing at her. His expression was serious and concerned. 'It got away from Monty,' she said, almost wailing like a little kid. *Waa-waa-waa.* 'It—it went under the sofa.'

He gave her freezing hands a warm squeeze. 'I'll deal with it, or at least Cricket and I will.'

'Cricket?'

The little dog at Flynn's feet yapped and spun around on his back legs as if on cue. He was not the sort of dog she was expecting someone like Flynn to own. She had expected some classy, Crufts-standard, purebred Malamute, a regal Great Dane or a velvet-smooth German pointer. Cricket wasn't any bigger than a child's football, was of indeterminate breed and looked like something out of a science fiction movie. His wiry coat was a caramel brown with little flecks of white that stood up at odd angles like they had been stuck on as an afterthought. He had one ear that stood up and one that flopped down, a thin, wiry tail that curled like a question mark over his back and a lower jaw that stuck out a few millimetres like a drawer that hadn't been shut properly.

'My right-hand man,' Flynn said. 'An expert at rodent-ectomies.'

Kat was almost limp with relief. 'I'd be ever so grateful.'

'Do you want to wait at my house while we get the business end of things sorted?'

Another groundswell of relief nearly knocked her off her feet, as if all her bones had been taken out of her body. 'You wouldn't mind?'

He smiled and looped her arm through one of his. 'Come this way.'

Kat was beyond worrying about going all damsel-in-distress with him. She *was* in distress. She would have happily sat in an axe murderer's house rather than face that…that creature under the sofa.

Besides, it was a perfect opportunity to have a look around Flynn's house while he wasn't there.

He unlocked the door and led her inside, telling her to make herself comfortable and that he'd be back soon. Cricket bounced at Flynn's feet as if he knew he was in for some blood sport. *Eeeww.*

Once they were gone Kat had a peep around. It was much the same layout as the Carstairses' house next door but, while the Carstairses' was a family home with loads of photos and family memorabilia, there was nothing to show Flynn's family of origin. There wasn't a single photo anywhere. There were some quite lovely works of art, however. And some rather gorgeous pieces of antique furniture that suggested he was a bit of a traditionalist, rather than a man with strictly modern taste.

Kat found his study next door to the sitting room, which had a beautiful cedar desk and leather Chesterfield chair. There was a black Chesterfield sofa set in front of the floor-to-ceiling bookshelves. The titles went from thick law tomes to the classics and history, with a smattering of modern titles, mostly crime and thrillers.

She went back into the sitting room and sat down at the grand piano that was set to one side of the room near the windows. She put her fingers to the keys, but all she could tinkle out was a nursery rhyme or two—but not Three Blind Unmentionables. Not exactly Royal Albert Hall standard, she thought with an embittered pang at what she could have had if her father had provided for her during her childhood. No doubt the Ravensdale siblings were all accomplished musicians. They had gone to fabulous schools and been taken on wonderful holidays with no expense spared.

What had she had?

A big, fat nothing. Which was why it was so hard to get established now. She was years behind her peers. She hadn't had acting lessons until recently because she couldn't afford them. She still couldn't afford a voice coach. A Scottish accent was fine if that was what a play called for. But she needed to be versatile, and that came with training, and training was hideously expensive—at least, the good quality stuff was. She could join some amateur group but she didn't want to be stuck as an extra in some unknown play in some way-out suburb's community hall.

She wanted to be at the West End in London.

It had been her goal since she was a kid.

It wasn't about the fame. Kat didn't give a toss for the fame. It was about the acting. It had always been about the acting, of getting into character in real time. About being onstage. About being in that electric atmosphere of being engaged with a live audience, seeing their reactions, hearing them gasp in shock, laugh in amusement or cry with heartfelt emotion. It wasn't the same, acting on a film set. The sequences were shot out of order. The camera had to come to you rather than onstage when you had to project your character to the audience.

That was what she loved. What she lived for, dreamed of, hungered after like a drug.

But there was another side to acting she found therapeutic. Cathartic, even. Stepping into a role was the chance to step away from her background. Her hurt. Her pain. Her shame.

The sound of Flynn's return made Kat scoot away from the piano and sit on one of the plush sofas, hugging a scatter cushion as if she had been there for the last half-hour.

Cricket came in with a panting smile, looking up at his master as if to say, 'Aren't I clever?'

'All sorted,' Flynn said.

Kat glanced at the dog's mouth to see if there was any trace of the murderous act that had gone on next door. 'Is it dead?' she asked, looking back at Flynn.

'Your visitor has gone to the great, big cheese shop in the sky.'

Her shoulders went down in relief. 'I can't thank you enough.'

Flynn looked at her for a beat. 'There is one way.'

Kat sprang to her feet. 'No. No way. You can't

blackmail me into seeing my father. Anyway, you said the wretched thing was dead. You can't bring it back to life to twist my arm.'

'It was worth a try, I thought.' He moved over to a drinks cabinet. 'Fancy a drink to settle your nerves?'

She wanted to say no but somehow found herself saying yes. 'Just a wee one.'

He handed her a Scotch whisky. 'From the home country.'

Kat took the glass from him, touching him for the second time that evening, but this time skin to skin. Something tight unfurled in her belly. 'Do you live here alone?' she asked to disguise her reaction to him.

'Yes.'

'No current girlfriend?'

His dark eyes glinted. 'I'm currently in the process of recruiting.'

Kat tried not to look at his mouth but it felt like an industrial-strength magnet was pulling her gaze to that stubble-surrounded sensual curve. 'How's that working out for you?'

'I have high hopes of filling the vacancy soon.'

'What are your criteria?' She gave him a pert look. 'Breathing with a pulse?'

Amusement shone in his gaze. 'I'm a little more selective than that. How about you?'

'What about me?'

'Are you dating anyone?'

Kat raised one of her brows in an arc. 'I thought you knew everything there was to know about me.'

'Not quite everything,' he said. 'But I know you've been single for a couple of months.'

How did he know? Or did he think no one would *want* to date her? Wasn't she up to his well-heeled standards? What was it about her that made him think she had 'single' written all over her? Surely he couldn't tell she hadn't had sex in ages. That was just plain impossible. No one could tell that... *Could they?* Or had he somehow found out about that stupid affair with Charles—the man who had conveniently forgotten to mention he had a wife—which had kicked off her celibacy pact? 'You know?' she said. 'How?'

He gave a light shrug of one of his shoulders. 'Just a feeling.'

'I thought lawyers relied on evidence, not feelings.'

His mouth slanted again. 'Sometimes a bit of gut instinct doesn't go astray.'

Kat moved her gaze out of reach of his assessing one. 'Your place looks like it's much the same layout as next door. Have you lived here long?'

'Seven years,' he said. 'I have another place in the country.'

Kat mentally rolled her eyes. 'Only one?'

He gave a low, deep chuckle that did strange things to the base of her spine, making it go all loose and wobbly. 'I like collecting things. Property is one of them.'

'Does it make you happy, having all that disgusting wealth to throw around?'

Something at the back of his gaze shifted. 'It's satisfying to have something that no one can take away.'

'Did you grow up with money?'

'My parents weren't wealthy by any means but they were comfortable.'

Kat looked at the gorgeous artwork hanging on the walls. None of them were prints. All were originals. One of them was surely a Picasso? 'They must be very proud of what you've achieved.'

He didn't answer for a moment. 'They enjoy the benefits of my success.'

She turned to look at him, wondering what was behind his cryptic response. 'Are you close to them?'

'I live my life. They live theirs.'

His expression had a boxed-up look about it. What was it about his family that made him so guarded? 'Do you have any brothers or sisters?' she asked.

'Two younger brothers.'

'What do they do?'

'Felix is a plumber and Fergus is a builder, like my father in Manchester,' he said. 'My mother stopped work when I came along. But now she does the bookwork and accounts for my father and brothers. She's made quite a career of it.'

Kat was surprised to hear he was originally from Manchester. He had no trace of the regional accent at all. But then, maybe he could afford a voice coach. 'How long have you lived in London?'

'Since I was ten,' he said. 'I won a scholarship to the same school the Ravensdale twins went to. I ended up spending more time at school than with my family.'

'Neither of your brothers got scholarships?'

'No.'

'Were they jealous?'

His mouth twisted. 'They're not the academic type. They both left school as soon as they could get an apprenticeship.'

'You don't sound like you have much in common with them.'

'I don't.'

Kat shifted her lips from side to side, wondering why he was so different from the rest of his family. His father and younger brothers were tradesmen and yet he was one of London's top lawyers, known for his incisive mind and clever wit. Had his stellar career trajectory made him an alien to his family? Had his educational opportunities created a chasm between him and his family that could not be bridged? Or was he just one of those people who didn't have time for family—an unsentimental man who wanted to make his own way in the world without the ties of blood?

There were no photos of his family around that she could see. Unlike the Carstairses' house next door, where just about every surface was covered in sentimental shots of happy family life. Flynn's house was more like a showcase house out of a home and lifestyle magazine. The luxurious decor spoke of unlimited wealth, yet it wasn't overdone. There was a sophisticated element to the placement of every piece of antique furniture, hand-woven carpet and the beautifully crafted soft furnishings.

She wasn't the sort of girl to get her head turned by a good-looking man. But something about Flynn made her senses go a little crazy. She was aware of him in a way she had never been aware of another man. She felt his proximity like a radar signal in her body. Every nerve was registering exactly where he was in relation to her. Even that first day, when he had come to her café and introduced himself, her body had responded with a shockwave of visceral energy. When his gaze met hers that first time she had felt a lightning-bolt reaction, like she was being zapped with a stun gun. She had felt it humming through her blood, an electric buzz that centred deep in her core. He had a sensual power about him way beyond any other man she had encountered before.

The thought of him touching her again was strangely exciting. He had nice hands, broad and square with long fingers and neat nails. He had a sprinkling of dark hair over the back of them that came from beneath the cuffs of his cashmere sweater, which made her imagination go wild, wondering where else it was sprinkled over the rest of his body. Would he be one of those men who man-scaped? Or would he be *au naturel*?

Cricket came and sat in front of her with a beseeching look on his face. Kat bent down and ruffled his funny little ears. 'How long have you had this adorable little guy?'

'I got him at Christmas.'

Kat looked up at Flynn. 'Where did you get him? Is he a rescue dog?'

Again he seemed to hesitate before he answered. 'You could say that.'

Kat frowned. 'What do you mean?'

He put his glass down but she noticed he hadn't drunk more than a sip or two. 'My mother has this habit of collecting cute strays but when they're no longer cute she gets rid of them.'

Kat heard the faint trace of bitterness in his tone. Was there more to the dog story than he was saying? Did it have something to do with his childhood? His relationship with his mother? His family? 'I always wanted a dog but we could never afford one while I was growing up,' she said. 'And we always lived in flats.'

'You could have one now, couldn't you?'

She straightened and glanced at him where he was leaning against the piano. 'I don't have the sort of lifestyle to own a dog. I move around a lot in search of acting work.'

'Anything on the horizon for you?'

Kat wasn't sure she wanted to tell him too much in case he told Richard Ravensdale. She wanted that part in the play on her own acting merit, not because of her famous father's influence. 'Not much.'

'Have you always wanted to be an actor?'

'Ever since I was old enough to know what acting was,' she said. 'I was cast as a donkey in a nativity play in primary school. I'll never forget the feeling I got when I looked out at that sea of faces. I felt like I had come home. They had to drag me off when it was over. I didn't want the play to end. Of course, my mother would've known why it was such a passion in me, but she never told me, not until a couple of days before she died. If anything she tried to discourage me from acting. She didn't even let me take dancing classes. Not that we could've afforded them, of course.'

Flynn was looking at her with a thoughtful expression on his face. 'It must have come as a big shock to find out who your father was. How had she settled your curiosity before then about who had fathered you?'

'She told me she didn't know who he was,' Kat said. 'When I was old enough to understand, she said she'd had a one-night stand with someone and never saw or heard from him again. I believed her because she kind of lived like that while I was growing up. She had men come and go all the time. None of her relationships lasted that long. She married at eighteen soon after she left home but they divorced before she was twenty. She wasn't all that lucky in the men department. She attracted the wrong sort of guy. She wasn't a great judge of character.' *Not that I can talk.*

'Were you close to her?'

Kat liked to think she had been to a point, but with her mother keeping such a secret from her for so long she wondered whether she had imagined their relationship to be something it was not in order to feel more normal. She was nothing like her mother in personality. Her mother had lacked ambition and drive. She hadn't seemed capable of making a better life for herself. She'd had no insight into how she'd kept self-sabotaging her chance to get ahead. Kat was the opposite. She was uncompromising in the setting and achieving of goals. If she put her mind to something, she would let nothing and no one stand in her way.

'I loved her, but she frustrated me because she didn't seem capable of making a better life for herself,' Kat said. 'She didn't even seem to want to. She cleaned hotel rooms or worked in seedy bars ever since she left home after a row with her parents as a teenager. She didn't even try to move up the ranks or try to train for something else.'

*What was she doing?* She wasn't supposed to be getting all chummy with him. What had made her spill all that baggage out? Was it because he had rescued her from the unwelcome visitor next door? Was it because he hadn't made fun of her about her phobia? Unlike a couple of her mother's dodgy boyfriends, who had found it great sport to see her become hysterical and paralysed with fear.

She rarely spoke to anyone of her background. Even her closest friend Maddie only knew the barest minimum about her childhood. Life had been tough growing up. Kat had always felt like an outsider. She had been the kid with the hand-me-down clothes; the one with the shoes that had come from a charity shop; the one with the home haircut, not the salon one. The kid who'd lived in run-down flats with lots of unwelcome wildlife. Money had always been tight, even though there had been ways her mother could have improved their circumstances. She sometimes wondered if her mother's lack of drive had made *her* all the more rigidly focused and uncompromisingly determined.

Flynn still had that contemplative expression on his face. 'You're so much like your father it's uncanny. He had his first start in theatre at the age of five too. Both he and Elisabetta talk of the buzz of being onstage in front of a live audience. It's like a drug to them. They don't feel truly alive without it.'

Kat wasn't so sure she wanted to be reminded of how like Richard Ravensdale she was. She had his green-grey eyes and dark-brown hair, although her natural copper highlights were from her mother. She used to be quite pleased with her looks, thanking her lucky stars she had a good face and figure for the theatre. But now they felt more like a burden. It was a permanent reminder of how her mother had been exploited by a man who had used her and cast her away once he was done with her.

She didn't fool herself that her mother had loved Richard and his abandonment had set her life on the self-destructive course it had taken. Her mother had already been well on her way down the slippery slope when she'd met Richard. It was more that Richard was one of many men who had used and abused her mother, fulfilling her mother's view of herself as not worthy of being treated with respect and dignity—messages she had heard since childhood. Kat had asked her mother just before she died why she hadn't made contact with Richard in later years to tell him he had a child. Her mother had told her it had never occurred to her. She had taken the money he'd offered and, as far as she was concerned, that was the end of it. It was typical of her mother's lack of drive and purpose. She'd let life happen to her rather than take life by the throat and wring whatever opportunities she could out of it.

'I'm not going to meet him, so you can put that thought right out of your mind,' Kat said.

'But he could help you get established in the theatre,' Flynn said. 'Why wouldn't you want to make the most of your connection to him?'

'It might be the way you lawyers climb the career ladder, by using the old boys' network, but I prefer to get there on my own,' Kat said. 'I don't need or want my father's help. He wasn't around when I needed it most and as far as I'm concerned it's way too late to offer it now.'

'What if it's not help he's offering?' he said. 'What if he just wants to get to know you? To have some sort of relationship with you?'

'I don't want to get to know him,' Kat said. 'I don't need a father. I've never had one before so why would I want one now?'

'Do you have any family now your mother's gone?'

Kat didn't like thinking of how alone in the world she was now. Not that she hadn't always felt alone anyway; but somehow having no living relative now made her feel terribly isolated, as if she had been left on an island in the middle of a vast ocean with no hope of rescue. Her grandparents had died within a couple of years of each other a few years back and, as her mother had been an only child, there were no aunts, uncles or cousins.

The Christmas just gone had been one of the loneliest times in her life. She had sat by herself in a damp and cold bedsit eating tuna out of a can, trying not to think of all the warm, cosy sitting rooms where families were gathered in front of the tree unwrapping gifts, or sitting around the dining table to a sumptuous feast of turkey and Christmas pudding. To have no backup, no sense of a safe home-base to go to if things turned sour, was something she had never really grown up with, but it didn't mean she didn't long for it— that sense of belonging, the family traditions that gave life a sense of security, of being loved and connected to a network of people who would look out for each other.

'There's just me,' she said. 'But I prefer it that way. I don't have to remember any birthdays or buy anyone expensive Christmas presents.'

The edge of Flynn's mouth tipped up in a wry smile. 'Always a silver lining, I guess.'

A small silence ticked past.

His eyes did a slow perusal of her face, finally lowering to her mouth and lingering there for an infinitesimal moment. The air felt charged, quickened by the current of sensual energy that arced between them.

Mutual attraction. Unmistakable. Powerful. Tempting.

Kat had been aware of it the first time they'd met. She was acutely aware of it now. She felt it in her body—the way her skin tightened and then lifted away from the scaffold of her skeleton; the way her breasts tingled as if preparing for his touch. Her insides quavered with a flicker of longing, shocking her because she had always been slow to arousal. She loved the intimacy of sex, of touching and being needed, but it always took her *so long* to get there.

But in Flynn's presence her body went on full alert, every erogenous zone flashing as if to say, 'Touch me!' Even the weight of his gaze on her mouth was enough to set her lips buzzing with sensation. She sent the tip of her tongue out to try and damp down the tingling but his hooded gaze followed every millimetre of movement, ramping up the tension in the air until she felt a deep, pulsing throb between her legs that echoed in her womb.

'Would you like to stay here tonight?' he said.

Kat laughed to cover how seriously tempted she was. 'I think I'll take my chances with the wildlife next door.'

'I wasn't asking you to sleep with me.'

Kat wished she could control the blush that filled her cheeks. A blush not so much of embarrassment, but of wanting what she wasn't supposed to want. And knowing he knew it. 'I'm not interested either way.'

'Liar,' he said. 'You were interested the moment I walked into that café that day with that cheque. That's why you haven't dated anyone since October.'

Kat wondered how on earth he had found out that information. Did he have someone tailing her? Keeping tabs on her? The last thing she wanted was anyone to find out she had mistakenly dated a married man. Her fledging career would be sabotaged if her affair with Charles Longmore were leaked in the press. Thankfully her partner in crime and grime was too frightened of his wife finding out to do his own press leak and cash in on her newfound fame as Richard Ravensdale's love child. 'I haven't dated because I made a celibacy pact with my best friend. We're off men until February.'

His eyes smouldered. 'I'll wait.'

Kat arched her brows. 'You don't strike me as a particularly patient man.'

'I know how to delay gratification,' he said. 'It makes the final feast all the more satisfying.'

No wonder he was a force to be reckoned with in court. He had a way with words that would leave most people's heads spinning.

But Kat was not most people. She too could delay gratification. Not only delay it but postpone it indefinitely. 'Don't set the table too early,' she said. 'Your guest might not show up.'

'Oh, she'll show up,' Flynn said with another glint in those bedroom eyes. 'She won't be able to stop herself.'

# CHAPTER FOUR

IT WAS SNOWING in earnest when Flynn walked Kat back to the house next door. Even though it was only a few metres, she was conscious of his tall, warm body walking beside her along the footpath. In her flat shoes she barely came up to his shoulder. She didn't like admitting it but their playful banter was something she found intensely stimulating. Sparring with him was like being involved in a fast-paced fencing match. She had to be on her guard every second.

She wondered if he would come into the café tomorrow. A little spurt of excitement flashed through her at the thought of seeing him again. She didn't want to be attracted to him, or to even like him, but the way he had handled the 'rodent-ectomy' as he called it had lifted him in her estimation. She still couldn't get over the fact he hadn't mocked her for her phobia. It had been a perfect opportunity to tease her. But instead he had simply dealt with the problem with surprising expertise and tact, as if it were perfectly normal for her to be squeamish about removing an unwanted creature from beneath the sofa.

Kat unlocked the door and turned to look up at him through the falling snow. 'Thanks for tonight.'

'You're welcome,' he said. 'I closed the cat flap, by the way. I put some duct tape over the catches. I think Monty must've worked them loose. He's a smart cat.'

Kat couldn't stop looking into his dark brown eyes with their thick fringe of lashes. Every now and again his gaze would flick to her mouth, the contact of his gaze making her lips feel tingly. 'Thanks for not making fun of me.'

His brow furrowed like a series of tide lines on a seashore. 'About what?'

'My silly phobia.'

He blinked away some snow and smiled, the flash of his white teeth making her stomach do a jerky little somersault. 'I used to be scared of the dark when I was kid. I slept with a night-light on for years. I got an awful ribbing about it at boarding school but eventually I got over it.'

'I can't imagine you being scared of anything.'

There was a long beat of silence.

Kat looked at his mouth—the way it was curved, the way his dark stubble surrounded it, the way his lean jaw with the sexy cleft in his chin made her ache to trail her fingertips over its rough surface. She sent the tip of her tongue out over her lips, watching with bated breath as his eyes tracked its journey. Her awareness of him sharpened. His stillness. As if he were waiting for her to make the first move. It had been months since she had felt a man's lips on hers. Months since she had felt a man's arms gather her close and remind her of how good it felt to be wanted. Needed.

Flynn's hands came down on the tops of her shoulders as softly as the snow cascading around them. His head came down, his foggy breath mingling with hers in that infinitesimal moment before contact. And yet, he didn't make that final contact. He hovered there as if he knew she would be the first to break.

*If you kiss him, you lose.*

*But I want to kiss him.*

*Yes, but he knows that, and that's why he's waiting.*

*I haven't been kissed in months.*

*He probably knows that too.*

*But it's been so long, I've almost forgotten what it feels like to be a woman.*

*If you kiss him, you might not be able to stop.*

Back and forth the battle with Kat's conscience and her flagging willpower went. And the whole time Flynn waited. She put a hand on his chest, then both hands. His coat was soft and warm to touch, but then, who could go past cashmere? Beneath the luxurious fabric she could feel the outline of his toned muscles. If she took a step, even half a step, she would be flush against his pelvis.

Even without closing that tiny distance she knew he was aroused. She *sensed* it. His body was calling out to hers, signalling to her, stirring hers to send the same message back. She became aware of her breasts, the way they seemed to swell, to prickle, to tingle. She became aware of her breathing; the way it stopped and started in little hitches and flows, swirling in a misty fog in front of her face, mixing intimately with his. She became aware of the pulsing throb between her legs, that most secret of places that ached for fulfilment. *Baboom. Baboom. Baboom.* The blood in her veins echoed the frantic need coursing through her.

'If you don't make up your mind soon, we're both going to freeze to death on this doorstep,' Flynn said.

Kat dropped her hands from his chest and stepped back. 'You thought you'd won that, didn't you?'

His glinting eyes and crooked smile made her insides twist and coil with lust. 'It's only a matter of time before I do.'

She gave him a scornful look. 'Dream on, Carlyon.'

His eyes darkened as if the challenge she'd laid before him privately excited him. 'Something you should know about me—I *always* win.'

Now it was Kat getting excited. She *loved* proving people wrong. It ramped up her determination. It fuelled the fire in her belly. If anyone said she *couldn't* do something, she made it her business to *do* it. If anyone said she *would* do something, she made sure she *didn't*.

Although there was a part of her that recognised the challenge of resisting Flynn Carlyon was right up there, as far as difficult challenges went. But as long as she kept her distance she would be home free. 'I'm sure that arrogance works well for you in court but it makes absolutely no impression on me,' she said.

He reached out his gloved hand and traced a fingertip along the surface of her bottom lip. 'I've thought about kissing you since the first day I met you.'

*Me too! Me too!* Kat kept her features neutral in spite of the excited leap of her pulse. 'I wouldn't have thought I was your type.'

His gaze went to her mouth as if savouring the moment when he would finally claim it. 'You're not.'

*Why the heck not?* 'Not used to slumming it, then?'

His brows came together, forming a two-fold

pleat between his eyes. 'Is that how you see yourself?'

It was how others saw her. She had been the victim of classism since she'd been old enough to know what it was. Having a charwoman and barmaid for a mother didn't exactly get her high enough on the social ladder to suffer vertigo. 'I know what side of the tracks I come from,' Kat said. 'It's certainly not the same side as you.'

His frown was still pulling at his brow, as if invisible stitches were being tugged beneath his skin. 'I wouldn't know about that.' Then after a slight pause he added, 'I don't actually know who my parents are.'

Kat frowned in confusion. 'But you said your father is a builder and your mum is—'

'They're not my real parents.'

She looked at him blankly. 'Not your real parents… Oh, are you adopted?'

Something in his eyes became shuttered. His mouth was flat. Chalk-white flat. I-wish-I-hadn't-said-that flat. But, after a moment of looking at her silently, he finally released a breath that sounded as if he had been holding it a long time. A lifetime. 'Yes. When I was eight weeks old.'

'Oh…I didn't realise. Have you met your birth mother?'

He gave a twist of a smile that didn't reach his eyes. 'No.'

'Have you gone looking?'

'There's no point.'

'Why?' Kat said. 'Don't you want to know who she is? Who both your parents are?'

He huddled further into his coat as the snow came down with a vengeance. Kat got the feeling he was withdrawing into himself, not because of the cold but because he'd obviously revealed far more than he'd wanted to reveal. 'I've kept you long enough,' he said. 'Go inside before you catch your death. Good night.'

She watched him stride through the white flurry of snow back to his house. He didn't look back at her even once.

He unlocked his front door and disappeared inside, the click-click sound of the lock driving home as clear as if he had said, 'Keep Out.'

\* \* \*

Flynn closed the door with a muttered curse. *What the hell were you thinking?* He wasn't thinking; that was the trouble when he was around Kat Winwood. He didn't think when he was around her. He *felt.* What was wrong with him, spilling all like that? He never talked about his adoptive family.

*Never.*

Cricket came slinking up on his belly as if he sensed Flynn's brooding mood. He bent down to ruffle the dog's ears. 'Sorry, mate. It's not you. It's me.'

Even his friends Julius and Jake Ravensdale knew very little of his background. They knew he was adopted but they didn't know he was a foundling. A baby left on a doorstep. No note pinned to him to say who he was and whom he belonged to. No date of birth. No mother or father to claim him. No grandparents.

Nothing.

That sense of aloneness had stayed with him. It was deeply embedded in his personality—

the sense that in life he could only ever rely on himself.

Even his adoptive parents had lost interest in him once they had conceived their own biological children. Flynn remembered the slow but steady withdrawal of his parents' attention, as Felix and Fergus had taken up more and more of their time. He remembered how on the outside he felt at family gatherings, where both sets of grandparents would dote on his younger brothers but pay little or no attention to him. The blood bond was strong; he understood it because he longed to have it. He ached to have knowledge of who he was and where he had come from.

But it was a blank.

*He* was a blank.

He was a man without a past. No history. No genealogy. No way of tracing the family he had been born into. In spite of extensive inquiries at the time of his abandonment, no one had come forward. He had spent years of his life wondering what had led his mother to leave him like a parcel on that doorstep. Why hadn't she wanted to keep him? Why had she felt she had no choice but to leave him on a cold, hard doorstep of a stranger's house? He had been less than a week old. His birth hadn't been registered. It was as if he had come out of nowhere.

What had happened to his mother since? Had she had more children? Who was his father? Had his mother and father loved each other? Or had something happened between them that had made it impossible for his mother to envisage keeping the baby they had conceived? Did his father even know of his existence? The thoughts of his origins plagued him. He couldn't look at a baby without thinking of what had led his mother to abandon him.

It was one of the reasons he hadn't pursued a long-term relationship since Claire. Back in his early twenties he had wanted to fill the hole in his life by building a future with someone, by having a family of his own. When Claire had had a pregnancy scare a couple of months into their relationship, he had proposed on the spot. The thought of having his own family, of having that solid unit, had been a dream come true. But when Claire had found out she wasn't pregnant a couple of days later she'd ended their engagement. Her rejection had felt like another doorstep drop-off.

He hadn't been able to commit to another long-term relationship since. To have his hopes raised so high only to have them dashed had made him wary about setting himself up for another disappointment. Not knowing who he was made him worried about who he might become. What if he didn't have it in him to be a good father? What if there was some flaw in his DNA that would make him ill-suited as a husband and father?

But now, as he was in his thirties and he saw friends and colleagues partnering and starting their parenting, he felt that emptiness all the more acutely. With Julius and Holly married now, Jake and Jaz engaged and Miranda and Leandro preparing for their wedding in March, he was the last man standing.

Alone.

Why had he told Kat Winwood, of all people? Or was it because he saw something in her that reminded him of himself? Her tough-girl exterior. Her take-no-prisoners attitude. Her steely self-reliance. Her feisty determination to win at all costs.

Everything about her stirred his senses into overload. Her sexy little body. Even her starchy stiffness when she was stirred up excited him. Her beautiful eyes, the colour of sea glass, fringed with long, black lashes that reminded him of miniature fans. Her pearly white skin, luminescent and without a single blemish, not even a freckle. Her rich dark-brown hair, with its highlights of burnished copper, that fell to just past her shoulders in a cascade of loose waves. Her flowery perfume—a hint of winter violets, lilacs and something else that was unique to her.

From the first moment he'd met her he had wondered what her lips would feel like against his own. He lay awake at night thinking about her. Imagining what it would be like to make love to her. He wasn't being over-the-top confident to think she was attracted to him. He could sense it in the way she kept looking at his mouth, as if a force was drawing her gaze there against her will. Even when she looked at him with those intelligent, defiant eyes he could see the flare of her pupils and the way her tongue sneaked out to moisten her luscious mouth. He enjoyed making her blush. It showed she wasn't quite as immune to him as she made out. He enjoyed sparring with her. The sexy banter was like foreplay. He got hard just thinking about it.

Every cell in his body delighted in the challenge she was laying before him. He thrived on the chase. The conquest was his lifeblood. It energised him. It excited him to think she was playing so hard to get. He was tired of the easy conquests. He could pull a date with just a look. It had lost its appeal. He wanted more. More depth, more intellectual stimulation, more time to explore the chemistry that sizzled and crackled between them.

Her strong will constantly clashed with his but that was what he found so attractive about her. She wasn't going to let anyone walk over her, or at least not without a fight.

Her indomitable stance on not meeting her father was a way of taking control—of being in charge. Richard had hurt her mother, Kat wanted justice and this was her way to get it. She was intent on punishing her father but what she didn't realise was, in the end, she was punishing herself and her half-siblings.

But Flynn wasn't going to stop until he had achieved what he'd set out to achieve. He wanted Kat Winwood at that party.

He wanted Kat Winwood, period.

Kat watched from an upstairs window the next morning as Flynn took his little dog Cricket for an early morning walk. He must have been up first thing to shovel the snow from his footpath. But then she looked down at hers and saw it was clear as well. A warm, oozy sort of feeling spread through her insides. Had he done that for her?

He was rugged up in coat, hat and gloves and he had dressed Cricket in a little padded coat that only left his ridiculous tail, odd ears and stumpy little legs on show. She watched as the dog bounced around him with glee, his little feet stirring up the powdery snow like a miniature snow machine. Flynn bent down and ruffled the dog's ears affectionately before they continued along the footpath.

What was the story with that crazy little dog? He had mentioned his mother had got tired of Cricket once he'd ceased to be cute. Had that happened with Flynn? Had his mother—both his parents—lost interest in him once their other sons had come along? Was that why he had been sent to boarding school? Were Flynn's brothers adopted too? Or had his parents conceived their own children after adopting him? It sometimes happened when a couple adopted a child after years of infertility.

So many questions were crowding her thoughts. She wanted to know more about him. She wanted to know everything about him.

*Oh no, here you go again.*

*What? I'm just interested in his background.*

*Sure you are.*

*I am!*

*You're interested in getting into bed with him. So much for your celibacy pact.*

*I'm not going to sleep with him. I just want to find out more about him.*

*You are so going to lose this.*

*I am not. I can resist him. I'm strong. I'm invincible. I'm disciplined.*

*You're toast.*

Kat was late getting back from working at the café as she had worked an extra shift because one of the waitresses had called in sick. The traffic was horrendous because of another heavy snowfall. The roads were slippery and tempers were becoming frazzled, including hers. And there were no parking spaces outside the Carstairs house. She had to do three tedious circuits before one became available in front of Flynn's BMW, as he had arrived just before her. *Typical. He gets the celebrity car spot while I'm driving around in circles for hours.* He was standing on the footpath retrieving some papers off the passenger seat as Kat drew alongside the car in front in order to reverse park. She tried not to be put off with him standing there watching her but every time she went to reverse back she was either too close to the car in front or too far from the curb.

Flynn tucked his papers under one arm and

came over to her driver's window, leaning down to speak to her. 'Do you want me to park it for you?'

Kat's pride came to her rescue. That was the second time he'd offered to park her car. What did he think she was? Useless? Sure, it was nice he'd scraped the snow away from her doorstep that morning, but she was perfectly capable of parking her car. If she let him do it for her, what else would she let him do? Allowing him to do stuff for her was a fast track into his bed and she was keeping off it. 'No thanks. I've got it.'

'I'll stand behind to guide you in. Take it slowly.'

Kat watched in the rear-view mirror as he positioned himself behind her car to stand in front of the BMW. She gave herself a pep talk. *You've parked a thousand times in spaces much tighter than this. Don't let him put you off. Just park the damn thing.* She put her indicator back on, positioned the wheels and then gingerly pressed her foot on the accelerator. She was doing brilliantly. *Yay!* The car was easing into the space like a dream but then another car flashed past, the driver called out something rude and Kat momentarily lost her focus. She forgot her foot was still on the accelerator until she felt the car go over a bump. The skin on her scalp shrank. She glanced behind her to see Flynn hopping about the footpath clutching one of his feet, a string of curse words coming out of his grimly set mouth.

Kat jumped out of the car, almost getting swiped by another car as it went past, spraying her with dirty, slushy snow. 'Oh, my God! Are you okay?'

He leaned one hand on the rear of her car as he put his foot to the ground, wincing as he tried to get it to take his weight. He frowned at her from beneath a single bar of eyebrows. 'Who taught you to park a car?'

Kat knew it wasn't the time to take umbrage with his tone but if he hadn't been there taunting her she would have parked the car just fine. Well, maybe. 'What were you doing standing *behind* my car? You should've stood on the footpath and directed me from there. That's what any sensible person would've done.'

'I wasn't going to stand by and watch you

plough your car into mine,' he said. 'I've only had it a month.'

He pushed himself away from her car and took a couple of steps but his mouth had white tips around the edges and he was barely able to put any weight on his foot. She chewed at her lips, wondering what she should do. She might be doing her level best to avoid him but she could hardly leave him to fend for himself, especially since she had been the one to run over his foot. 'Do you want me to call an ambulance or…or something?'

'That won't be necessary.'

Kat tried not to be put off by his clipped tone. He was in pain. Of course he would be brusque. 'I'm sorry…I didn't mean to hurt you. My tyres are a little bald and I—'

'Your tyres are *bald* and you're driving on them in this weather?' He glowered at her. 'Do you realise how dangerous that is? Not just to yourself but to other innocent people on the road?'

Kat put up her chin. It was all right for him to bang on about new tyres. He could afford to buy any brand of tyre he liked. He could afford to buy any *car* he liked. She had to make do with whatever she could afford. She couldn't do without a car when she had to go to auditions all over the country. 'I bet your foot isn't even hurt. I bet you're one of those men that get man flu. One sniffle and I bet you go to bed all day.'

He shook his head at her like a frustrated parent does a wilful child. 'You're freaking unbelievable.'

Kat spun on her heel and stalked off without another word. She was glad she'd run over his foot. It served him right. She would do it again if she had half a chance.

*Both feet.*

## CHAPTER FIVE

'BROKEN?' FLYNN ASKED, peering at the X-ray of his right foot that his friend Dr Joaquim Barrantes in A&E was showing him on the computer screen.

'In three places,' Joaquim said. 'How'd you do it again?'

Flynn gave him a speaking look. 'Don't ask.'

Joaquim grinned. 'So, how are things going with that hot little Scot? Got her to go out with you yet?'

'I'm working on it.'

'How many months has it been now?' Joaquim gave him a teasing look. 'Not like you to take so long to get down to business. You must be losing your touch.'

'I've changed my tactics,' Flynn said. '"Slowly but surely" is my new M.O.'

Joaquim nudged some crutches that were

propped against the gurney. 'Yeah, well, these will slow you down a bit. But you'll be fine with a bit of rest. You don't need it plastered, just a firm bandage and crutches for four weeks. The bones are small, but you don't want to compromise healing with too much weight on them in the early stages of recovery.'

*Crutches.* Flynn smothered a curse. What was that going to do to his credibility in court? Limping around on a pair of crutches didn't suit his image of being in control. But taking time off while his foot healed would be pointless. What could he do? He wasn't the sit-around-the-house type. It was not as though he could go skiing. He wouldn't even be able to head to somewhere warm. Walking on a beach or lounging around a resort pool on crutches wasn't his idea of fun. And spending time with his family in Manchester wasn't something he was keen to repeat after the Christmas debacle. And who was going to walk Cricket twice a day?

The cogs of Flynn's mind began to tick over. He wasn't averse to twisting the odd emotional blackmail screw when it suited him. Besides, Kat owed him something, surely? She might not have deliberately injured him but he was a firm believer in do the crime, do the time. And it would be rather entertaining to have her play nursemaid. He would be able to see her several times a day. Every morning. Every night.

Who knew what he could talk her into with that amount of close contact?

'What about driving?' Flynn asked his friend.

Joaquim shook his head. 'It would be fine if it wasn't your right foot but your insurance company wouldn't cover you if you drove with it until you've been given the all clear. Just as well you filthy rich lawyers can afford to catch cabs everywhere.'

'Funny,' Flynn said. 'But us rich lawyers are the people you overworked medicos turn to when your patients want to sue you.'

Joaquim tapped his fingers on the wooden desk he was standing next to. 'So far, so lucky.'

Kat was glancing out of the front window to see if the snow had stopped when she noticed a cab pulling up outside Flynn's house. Her stomach dropped when she saw Flynn get out on crutches, his foot heavily bandaged. *Crutches?* Oh, dear Lord! What had she done? Would he sue her? He was a lawyer. A high-profile one. She would be taken to the cleaners... Not that she owned anything, but still... The thought of wounding someone—anyone—was anathema to her. Now she'd had time to cool down, she realised how rude she had been. Acting as if it was his fault his foot had got run over.

It was *her* fault.

She was lousy at parking. She always had been. She needed to eat a big slice of humble pie even if she choked on it. She let the curtain drop back and raced out, only stopping long enough to put on a coat. The icy air burned her cheeks but she figured it would counter the hot blush currently residing there.

Flynn had not quite made it to his front door when she came up alongside him. 'Oh, my God!' she said. 'Is it broken?'

'In three places.'

'I'll pay your health costs.' She swallowed convulsively, mentally checking her bank account and wondering how she was going to follow through on her promise.

'Forget about it.'

'But surely I can do something?'

He seemed to consider her question for a moment, his eyes studying her face as if committing it to memory. 'Can you cook?'

'Yes, but—'

'Good,' he said. 'I'll need a meal each evening and lunch and dinner on weekends, unless I go out, which I very much doubt I'll be doing much of now I'm on these damn crutches.'

Kat frowned. 'Don't you have a housekeeper?'

'Only to clean the house once a week,' he said. 'I'll need help with shopping and walking Cricket and running errands. You up for it?'

She tried not to look resentful, given her role in his predicament, but she couldn't help feeling he was orchestrating things to suit his ends. But spending time with him in any capacity was surely asking for the sort of trouble she could do without.

He was too confident. Too sure of himself. Too darned sexy. *Yes, even on crutches.*

He did something to her female hormones. They started humming with excitement. They did cartwheels in her belly when his dark eyes locked on hers. When he looked at her mouth her insides quivered at the thought of those firm but sensual lips coming into contact with hers. Not that she would let that happen. If he thought he could win her over with seduction then he was in for a big let-down.

*You broke his foot on purpose.*

*I did not! It was an accident.*

*Now you'll have to spend hours with him, doing stuff for him. Acting like a wife.*

*I will not be like a wife. I'll walk the dog, put the rubbish out, pick up his dry cleaning and cook his meals... Eek! You're right—I'll be like a wife.*

'Isn't there someone else you can get to help you?' Kat said. 'It's not like you couldn't afford to pay someone.'

'You're the one who broke my foot. Why should I be out of pocket for an inconvenience you caused?'

Kat would have liked to call his bluff but he

was a high-powered lawyer and she was one job away from the dole queue. He was well within his rights to sue her for causing injury. She wouldn't stand a chance in defending herself, nor could she afford a defence lawyer to act on her behalf. Her space between a rock and a hard place had just got a little more cramped. Hippopotamus-in-a-hot-tub cramped. 'I don't suppose I have much choice.'

'That's settled, then. Why don't you come in now and I'll show you round the kitchen?' A glint appeared in his gaze and he added, 'I might even have an apron I can loan you—that is, unless you have one of your own?'

Kat gave him a beady look. 'No, funnily enough, that's one item that's missing from my wardrobe.'

As soon as Flynn opened the door Cricket came bowling out, spinning around Kat's legs, yapping volubly, bouncing up and down on his stubby little legs like his paws were on springs. She crouched down so she could pat him and got her faced licked for her trouble. 'Oh, you crazy little mutt.' She laughed and pulled back before he took off her make-up. 'Only a mother could love that little face.'

Kat looked up to see Flynn looking at her with a faraway look in his gaze. 'Sorry.' She got to her feet. 'That was a bit insensitive of me…'

He gave a brief smile. 'It's fine. He was a very cute puppy. Anyone would've fallen for him.'

Kat followed him and the dog inside. She took one of Flynn's crutches so he could take off his coat. She could feel the warmth of the hand rest where his fingers had just been, making her own hand tingle. She helped him take off his coat as if taking an explosive device from a would-be suicide bomber. She didn't touch his body, only the fabric of his coat, but she could feel the electric pulse of his proximity shoot through her body like a lightning zap. 'Are your brothers adopted too?'

He propped himself back on both crutches. For a moment she thought he was going to tell her to mind her own business. His dark eyes had a curtained look. A don't-bother-knocking-no-one's-going-to-answer look. But then his expression subtly changed. There came a slight relaxation of the muscles as if something tight and restricted inside his mind had loosened. 'No. My parents managed to conceive naturally three years after adopting me.'

Was that why he wasn't close to his family? Was that why he had been sent away to school? His parents hadn't needed him once they had created their own flesh and blood? He was like the cute little puppy that had failed to be cute once it grew up a bit and got a little more challenging to handle. 'Is that why you're not close to them?' Kat said. 'Did they treat you differently once they had their own kids?'

He gave a resigned lip-shrug. 'Sharing DNA with your kids is a powerful factor in bonding with them. Adoption works well when it works, but when it doesn't it can be a disaster.'

Kat's heart squeezed for the little boy he had been. How painful for him to have been shunted aside like a toy that no longer held its initial appeal. Small children picked up on the slightest change in dynamic with primary caregivers. The thought of Flynn recognising at such a young age he was no longer important to his parents must have had a devastating effect on him. 'Your adoptive parents shouldn't have treated you any differently,' she said. 'They made a commitment to you as a baby that was meant to be for life.'

He gave her a twisted smile that had a hint of sadness to it. 'It doesn't always work like that. Matching kids to parents isn't an exact science. I was a difficult baby, apparently. When my parents had Fergus and then Felix they realised it wasn't their parenting that was the problem—it was me. I simply didn't belong in that family.'

Kat frowned. 'I don't believe that for a second. They adopted you as a tiny baby. They should've bonded with you no matter what. You don't give up on a child just because it doesn't fulfil your expectations. A child is an individual. They have their own path to tread. It's the parents'—biological or adoptive—responsibility to make sure their child gets every opportunity to become the person they're meant to become.'

Cricket gave a loud yap, as if in agreement. Flynn smiled wryly as he scratched the dog's belly with the rubber end of his crutch. 'Not every kid gets that level of commitment, do they, Cricket?'

Kat chewed at her lip for a moment. 'You said the other day there was no point looking for your birth parents. What did you mean by that?'

He stopped scratching the dog and started hopping towards the kitchen. 'Cricket needs feeding. I usually take him out for half an hour morning and evening, after his breakfast and dinner.'

She followed him into the kitchen. 'Flynn, why won't you talk about your birth parents? You shut up like a clam with lockjaw every time I mention them.'

He pointed to the pantry with one of his crutches as if she hadn't spoken. 'His dry food's in there and his meat's in the fridge. There's more in the freezer.'

The drawbridge was up. She could see the tight muscles on his face. The set mouth. She had come too close and he was telling her not to come any closer. But the more he pushed her away the more she wanted to draw close. He was so much more than the arrogant my-way-or-the-highway man she had thought him on first appearances. He was deep. Deep and mysterious. Intriguing to the part of her that couldn't help feeling compassion for a fellow sufferer of the club of Not Belonging. 'Is your foot hurting you?' she said.

He rubbed his hand over his face loud enough for her to hear the rasp of his stubble. 'I had a couple of painkillers at the hospital. I might go and have a lie down. I'm feeling like a bit of a space cadet.'

'I'll sort out Cricket and then bring you up something to eat,' Kat said. 'Do you have a spare key so I can let myself back in?'

'There's one in the bowl on the hallstand. It's on a blue key ring.'

Kat let herself back in forty minutes later with Cricket panting at her feet. He had been a little darling, trotting by her side as if he had got first-class honours from obedience school. However, it had been a completely different story at the dog exercise area in the park. Cricket hadn't cared for the other dogs, especially the big ones. He'd strained at the leash and barked and snarled as if he'd been ready to rip them apart. It hadn't won him any friends. The other owners had quickly called their dogs back and given Kat looks, as if to say, 'Why don't you get control of your dog?'

It had been humiliating.

But for all that she couldn't help thinking it was a bit of a windfall having this one-on-one time with Cricket. The play she was auditioning for was A. R. Gurney's *Sylvia*, which was a play about a middle-aged married man who brought home a dog he found at the park, much to his wife's displeasure, because she wanted to enjoy their empty nest. Kat was auditioning for the role of Sylvia the dog, a wonderful part that was energetic and challenging on every level. A Canadian actor was playing the lead of Greg, the husband's role, but no one knew who was playing Kate, the wife, as it was apparently the director's secret. It would be announced once the auditions were over. An understudy would take the role until formal rehearsals started.

Kat wanted that role. It was a chance-in-a-lifetime role. A star-making role. Audiences loved Sylvia. It was the actor who played the dog that made or broke the performance. If she got that part it would be her chance to prove her mettle as an actor.

Kat tossed a salad and set it beside the fluffy cheese omelette she had made. Cricket followed at her heels as she carried it upstairs. She had no idea where Flynn's bedroom was but the layout was much the same as next door so she took a gamble. She found him fast asleep on the bed with one hand folded across his flat stomach and the other in a right angle flung back on the pillow at his head. His bandaged foot was propped on another pillow; the other one was still wearing a shoe—a black Italian leather zippered ankle boot. His handsome features were relaxed in sleep, giving him a vulnerable look that was at odds with his reputation as an intimidating courtroom king.

She approached the bed with caution, not wanting to wake him, but unable to stop herself from going closer. She leaned down to put the tray on the bedside table and then straightened to see if he had registered her presence. His eyelids flickered as if he was in the middle of a dream and his lips were slightly parted, enough for her to hear the soft, even rhythm of his breathing.

On an impulse she could neither explain nor control, Kat reached out and gently brushed her fingers down the stubble-shadowed landscape of his jaw. The slight catch of her softer skin on his raspy one made something slip sideways in her stomach, like a stockinged foot on a shiny floor.

He opened his eyes and reached for her hand at the same time, his fingers wrapping around the slim bones of her wrist like a steel bracelet. He gave her a slow smile. 'Changed your mind about that kiss?'

Kat tried to pull out of his hold but his fingers tightened just a fraction—a delicious fraction that set her nerves tingling. 'I—I was checking to see if you had a temperature. You can never be too careful with fractures. There can be internal bleeding and infection and you might—'

'Am I hot?'

Way, way too hot. Way too hot for her to handle. 'I brought you some dinner. Just leave the tray—I'll clear it away in the morning.'

He released her hand and patted the bed near his thigh. 'Sit. Stay and talk to me.'

*Don't do it.*

*Why not? He only wants to talk.*

*Yeah, right.*

*He needs some company. He's injured.*

*Not his mouth, or his hands, or his you-know-what. They're in perfect working order.*

Kat felt the usual tug of war inside her mind, not to mention inside her body. She knew she should leave but another part of her wanted to stay. He drew her interest in a way no other man had done before. There was something about him that made her flesh sing just by being in the same room as him—from breathing the same air as him. He had a potent effect on her senses. He made her aware of her femininity, of her needs— the needs that were proving rather difficult to ignore, especially when she was this close to him. Close enough to touch his face again, to trace the sensual contour of his tempting mouth. To lean down and press her lips to his and see what fireworks would happen—for they *would* surely happen. She knew it in her bones. 'Just for a minute, then…' She sat on the edge of the bed.

He surveyed her features for a moment. 'It was kind of you to stay and make me dinner. I wasn't sure you would.'

Kat gave a shrug. 'There's nothing to making an omelette.'

His thumb found her pulse and stroked over its frantic beat as his eyes held hers in a mesmerising lock. 'It's a pity we met the way we did. Perhaps if we'd met under different circumstances you wouldn't be sitting there but lying in here beside me.'

Kat felt a ripple of lust between her legs but disguised it by casting him a resentful glare. 'You cost me my job in that café.'

He gave a little grimace of remorse. 'I know. But I was lucky I didn't get burnt when you poured that coffee in my lap.'

She chewed at her lip when she recalled that day. Having Flynn show up at the café the day after her mother's funeral with that cheque from Richard Ravensdale had been like coarse salt rubbed into a festering wound. The thought of being paid to keep silent about something that should never have been a secret in the first place was an insult. So too was the fact that her father had sent his lawyer instead of coming to see her in person.

That hurt.

It shouldn't but it did. If her father wanted to have a relationship with her—a proper relationship—then why send someone else to set it up for him?

But, no, Richard had paid someone to pay her to keep her mouth shut about his dirty little affair with a hotel housemaid. Now Richard wanted to be a father to her. Why? To boost his popularity? To keep his fans happy? It certainly wasn't because he cared about her.

But Flynn had a point. If she and Flynn had met some other way she might well have considered getting involved with him. He was the most interesting man she had ever met. His looks made her go weak at the knees, but he was so much more than a good-looking man. She found his razor-sharp intelligence the biggest turn on. He was funny and charming, and yet there were layers to him, depths he kept hidden. Enigmatic depths that made her want to get as close as she possibly dared.

'I'm sorry about the coffee but it was all too much,' Kat said. 'I'd only just got back from Glasgow from the funeral. I didn't even know how anyone had found out about his affair with my mother. It was a shock to find it splashed all over the papers.'

'Apparently one of your mother's former work-mates let something slip to a journalist,' Flynn said. 'The rest, as they say, is history.'

'Sometimes I wish I hadn't agreed to that paternity test. But I wanted to know for sure.'

'At least you know who your father is. Lots of people never find out.'

Kat looked at him again. There was a slight frown pulling at his brow, as if he was thinking about something that pained him. Twice now she had tried to draw him out about his birth parents but he had shut off the conversation. Why was he being so stubborn about it? Lots of relinquished children managed to conduct loving relationships with their biological parents once contact was made. 'If your biological parents ever came looking for you would you want to meet them?'

His eyes didn't meet hers. 'I can't see it happening now. Not after thirty-four years.'

'It's never too late to give up hope.'

He gave her a movement of his lips that was almost a smile. 'That's exactly what your father keeps saying.'

Kat didn't want to think about the father she didn't want, and Flynn's father, whom he might never meet. In her mind the two situations were completely different. 'Is your foot troubling you?'

'Not much.'

She rose from the bed. 'I should let you have your food and go back to sleep.'

He captured her hand again, giving it a light squeeze that was perfectly timed with his on-off smile. 'Thanks.'

Kat bit her lip again as she looked at their joined hands. His skin was deeply tanned, as if he had been somewhere warm recently. She could see the paler band where his watch usually rested. His fingers were almost twice the thickness of hers, making her feel more feminine than she had in years. If she could just grow her nails instead of biting them back to the elbow she would feel even more feminine. 'I'm really sorry about your foot.'

But, when she looked back at him to see why he hadn't said anything, she saw he was soundly asleep.

Flynn swore as he came out of the shower the next morning. Not only had he overslept, which was going to make him late for his first client, the plastic bag he had wrapped around his foot hadn't done the job of keeping his bandage dry. And his foot was hurting. Badly. He limped out of the *en suite* to his bedroom with a towel around his hips to find Kat at his bedside collecting his tray from the night before.

She swung around and then quickly averted her gaze. 'Sorry. I thought you were still in the shower. I knocked but—'

'It's fine.' He reached for a pair of boxers and a shirt. 'I'm going to be late for work. Has Cricket been out yet?'

She kept her back turned to him as she straightened his bed, smoothing down the covers with meticulous precision, as if she did it for a living. 'Yes, I took him out first thing.'

'Why didn't you wake me?'

'I wasn't aware being an alarm clock was on my list of duties,' she said in a crisp tone.

'I got my bandage wet.'

She turned to look at him, her eyes giving a little flash. 'Poor baby.'

He clipped on his watch, snapping the catch in place. 'I haven't got time for breakfast. I have to brief a client before court. Can you hand me those trousers?'

'These?'

'No, the grey ones.'

'Here you go.'

Flynn winked at her. 'You'd make a great wife.'

She gave him an artic look. 'I have other ambitions.'

He slipped his belt through the lugs on his trousers whilst balancing on one crutch. 'You don't want to get married and have kids some day?'

'I want to establish my career first,' she said.

'Husbands have a way of getting in the way of career aspirations; kids even more so.'

Flynn wondered if she was being completely truthful. He had only met a handful of women who didn't want the whole package. He had wanted it himself until having it snatched away had made him reassess. But after he had come back to London on Christmas night after the usual palaver with his family—having rescued Cricket from being ignominiously dumped at the nearest dog shelter for almost certain euthanasia—the Carstairs family had invited him in for supper.

The difference in households had been nothing short of stunning. There was none of the stiffness and formality of his family, pretending to be comfortable with him when clearly they weren't. The Carstairses' kids, Josh and Bella, had run up to him and hugged him around his legs, grinning from ear to ear, excited beyond bounds he had come to join them. To see such unabated joy on their little faces had sent a rush of unexpected emotion to his throat, making him feel like he was choking on a pineapple. He had watched in silent envy as Neil and Anna had exchanged loving glances over the tops of the heads of their children who were miniature replicas of them.

It was fine now, being single and free to do what he liked, but what about in a few years' time? Would he still feel the same? Or would he feel a deep cavern of emptiness inside him where the love of a wife and family should have been? He was already tired of the dating scene. The thought of coming home to someone who wanted to be with him because they loved him, not because he was rich or well-connected, was something he couldn't stop thinking about lately.

It was like a door inside his mind he had thought he had closed and bolted had been prised open. A crack of light was shining through, illuminating the possibilities. Possibilities like kids to go with the dog he already had. He loved coming home to Cricket. Seeing that funny little face beaming with excitement at seeing him had shifted something inside him. It made him see what an alternative life could be like. A life where not just a scruffy little dog would bolt up the hallway to greet him but a couple of grubby-faced kids like

Josh and Bella. Kids who looked like him. Who carried the same DNA. Family was something he had seen as something other people had, not him. He was alone. Unattached. Without a blood bond.

*But what if he made one?*

He dismissed the thought, pushing it back behind the door in his mind, leaning his resolve against it to make sure it was closed.

'Can you choose me a tie?' Flynn said.

Kat went back to his wardrobe and selected a tie. 'Will this one do?'

'Perfect. Can you put it on for me?'

Her lips pursed. 'Why do I get the feeling you're making the most of this situation?'

He smiled as her hands looped the tie around his neck. This close he could smell her winter flowers fragrance as it danced and flirted with his senses. The temptation to press his mouth to hers was like a tug of war inside his body; every organ strained at the effort of keeping his willpower under control. 'Why do I get the feeling you'd like to strangle me?'

Her gaze went to his mouth. Her fingers worked on his tie but he could feel them tremble as they inadvertently touched the skin of his neck. His blood leapt at the contact, pulsing through his veins like rocket fuel. She took her bottom lip between her teeth in concentration—or was it because she was fighting an urge, the same urge he could feel barrelling through his body? She completed his tie and gave his chest a quick pat. 'There.' She gave him the briefest flash of a smile. 'All done.'

His gaze locked on hers, watching as the dark ink of her pupils in that sea of bewitching green widened. Watching too as the tip of her tongue came out and darted over the surface of her lips, the top first and then the bottom, leaving them moist, shining and tempting. His blood headed south, his groin swelling and tingling with the promise of contact. Any contact. He couldn't think of a time when he had wanted a woman more than her. But he wanted her to make the first move. She was oscillating; he could tell. The same battle he was fighting in his body was being played out over her features. Her gaze slipped again to his mouth. Her tongue did another circuit of her lips. Her breathing hitched just loud enough for him to hear it. He saw the rise and fall of her slender throat. He ached to press his lips to the thrumming pulse he could see hammering there. 'What have you got riding on this celibacy pact?' he asked.

She swallowed again. Audibly. 'Wh-why do you want to know?'

'Just wondering what's keeping your self-control in check.'

Her chin came up, her mouth pulled tight again. 'You think you're so damn irresistible, don't you?'

Flynn smiled at her. 'You want me *so* bad.'

Her eyes fired a round of ire at him. 'I. Do. Not. Want. You.'

'How many times do you reckon you'll have to say that to believe it?'

Her breath came out like a small explosion. 'You're unbelievable. You think just because every other woman you've ever smiled at fell at your feet that I will too. Well, guess what? I won't.'

'That's what the silly little celibacy pact is all about, isn't it?' Flynn said. 'You knew from the moment we met that we would end up in bed together so you thought of a plan to prevent it from happening. Cute plan, but it's doomed to fail.'

She laughed but it didn't sound authentic, more like someone acting as though they were amused when deep down they were anything but. 'No wonder those bones broke in your foot. They were probably weakened from carrying around your ego.'

'Speaking of my broken foot,' Flynn said. 'Can you carry my briefcase downstairs?'

She gave him a mutinous look, but then her gaze went to his crutches and she gave a tiny swallow. 'How will you get to work? You can't drive, can you?'

'Unfortunately, no.'

She bit her lower lip and glanced at his bandaged foot again. 'I could drive you if you—?'

'No.'

She gave him a steely glare. 'There's no need to be so emphatic about it.'

'I'll take my chances with a cab,' Flynn said. 'But don't worry—I'll keep the receipts for you.'

# CHAPTER SIX

FLYNN WASN'T HOME when Kat arrived later that day to take Cricket out for his evening walk. She refused to acknowledge the little slump in her spirits. What did she care if he wasn't home? It was better if she *didn't* see him, especially after seeing him all but naked this morning. Every time she thought of coming across him in his bedroom in nothing but a towel hitched around those lean hips her stomach somersaulted. His body was as attractive as his mind. Toned and tanned with muscles in all the right places. And his sexy frame was sprinkled with just enough masculine hair for her hormones to start fanning themselves.

But, when she walked back from the park with a panting Cricket at her side, she noticed more lights on in Flynn's house than she had left on when she had let herself in earlier. The front door opened before she could use the key Flynn had given her but it wasn't him standing there—it was Miranda Ravensdale. *Gulp.* Her half-sister. Kat knew it was Miranda as she had seen numerous photos of her and her brothers when the news of her existence had broken.

Miranda smiled shyly. 'Hi. I'm Miranda. I hope you don't mind us dropping in like this but when we heard Flynn broke his foot Jaz and I thought we'd better drop off a casserole or something. We won't stay long. We're just going, aren't we, Jaz?'

Before Kat could think of anything to say, another young woman appeared. 'Hiya.' Jasmine Connolly gave a beaming smile. 'So, we finally meet. Hey, Cricket.' She bent down and cuddled the dog, who was in a paroxysm of delight. 'What do you think of your new neighbour, huh? Isn't she a sweetheart to take you out for walkies?'

Why had Jaz made it sound as if Kat had taken the dog out as a Good Samaritan favour? Kat couldn't stop looking at Miranda, searching the young woman's elfin features for any likeness to her own. Her half-sister. A relative. Someone to belong to. Family. 'Erm…nice to meet you.'

Miranda bit her lower lip. 'Is it too awkward for you? I mean, we can leave now, can't we, Jaz?'

'But I thought we were going to stay and have dinner with Flynn?' Jaz said.

Kat saw the two exchange glances. 'I'm just dropping off Cricket,' she said into the little silence.

'Oh, won't you stay and have dinner with us?' Miranda's gaze was a wide, enthusiastic, welcome-to-the-family one. 'We made enough to feed an army. Two armies, the navy and the air force, actually. Julius and Jake aren't here, if that's what's worrying you. Julius and Holly are in Argentina just now and Jake's out with Leandro, my fiancé, at a work thing.'

Kat knew it would look churlish of her to refuse. But meeting her half-sister without warning had thrown her completely. No doubt Flynn was behind this impromptu meeting. Her fury at him boiled in her blood like caustic soda until her veins felt like they were going to bust. How dared he engineer a meeting she didn't want? Wasn't emotionally ready for? What if he'd invited her father? The whole freaking family? 'Where is Flynn?' she said.

'In the sitting room with his foot up,' Miranda said. 'I insisted he rest it. It's awfully bruised and swollen. I think he's been putting weight on it against doctor's orders. Some men make terrible patients.'

Kat peeled off her gloves, studying both girls with a watchful gaze. 'Did he tell you how he broke it?'

'He said he tripped down the stairs,' Jaz said. 'Not like him to be so clumsy, is it, Miranda?'

'No.' Miranda laughed self-deprecatingly. 'That's the sort of thing I would do, not Flynn.'

Kat opened and closed her mouth, stuck for something to say. Why hadn't he told the girls the truth? Why hadn't he exploited the situation? Why tell them he'd tripped when he could have told them *she* was responsible?

Jaz's grey-blue eyes began to dance. 'So, how long have you two been seeing each other?'

Kat straightened her shoulders. 'I'm not. We're not. I'm just—'

'House-sitting next door—yeah, yeah, yeah,' Jaz said, still grinning. 'Kind of convenient, huh?'

Kat elevated her chin, her mouth set in a prim Sunday school teacher line. 'Mr Carlyon recommended me to the Carstairs family next door. That is and will remain the only connection I have with him.'

Jaz was undaunted and gave Miranda a little elbow-nudge. 'Mr Carlyon? That's cute. And does he call you "Miss Winwood"?'

Kat glanced at Miranda, who was looking at her with big, soulful Bambi eyes. It occurred to her then that this meeting must be as tricky for Miranda as it was for her.

She was the interloper. The new half-breed sister. The shameful secret that had come to light after twenty-three years of silence. How awful must it be for Miranda to have to face the living and breathing evidence of her father's betrayal of his marriage vows? Miranda was no longer the baby sister, the youngest child. Kat had taken that position from her. The press had even gone as far to say Kat was the more beautiful of the sisters. Before that Miranda had always been compared to her glamorous mother and found lacking, and now she had a half-sister to be compared to. How did Miranda feel about that? Was she angry? Upset? Did she project that negative emotion on Kat?

Not so far as Kat could see. If anything, Miranda looked like she wanted to make a good impression. She looked like she was keen to establish a bond with her but was uncertain about how she would be received.

'What does a guy have to do to get a drink around here?' Flynn's deep voice called out from the sitting room.

Jaz turned on her heel and marched off to the sitting room. 'You're not supposed to drink when you're taking prescription painkillers,' she said.

Miranda looked at Kat with a shy grimace. 'I know this must be just awful for you…meeting me like this…I know you've not wanted any contact. I understand that. I really do. The whole situation is just ghastly for you but I do want us to be friends if at all possible. None of this is your fault. None of us blame you for it—well, apart from Mum, but let's not even go there.'

'Thanks.' Kat forced a smile. 'It's kind of weird but not awful. I've just needed some time to get my head around it all.'

Miranda's features relaxed ever so slightly. 'Please don't be offended by Jaz's teasing just now. She just wants everyone to be as happy as she is, now she and Jake have got engaged. You're the last Ravensdale to be single...I mean, not that you probably think of yourself as a Ravensdale or anything, but...' She bit down on her lip again and blushed. 'I'm sorry. I'm making such a dreadful hash of this. I always talk too much when I'm nervous.'

'I go quiet when I'm nervous,' Kat said.

Miranda's eyes bulged. 'Really? That's exactly like Julius. I can't wait until you meet the boys. They're awesome big brothers. They're really looking forward to meeting you. But only if you want to, of course. You mustn't feel pressured to meet Dad. He can be a bit overpowering.' She gave a little eye-roll. 'Not to mention Mum—but don't get me started.'

Kat felt her smile relax. 'She's actually one of my favourite theatre actors.'

'Really?'

'She's amazing onstage,' Kat said. 'She's spellbinding to watch live. I could watch her all day.'

Miranda did that lip-chewing thing again and a small frown pulled at her smooth forehead. 'I've always found my mother's fame a bit of a burden. I know she's supertalented and all that but sometimes I just wanted her to be a mum. A normal one, you know?'

Kat gave her a wry look. 'What's normal? My mum certainly wasn't a soccer mum.'

Miranda touched Kat's arm, those big brown eyes warm and compassionate as they held hers. 'I'm really sorry about your loss. You must miss her dreadfully.'

Kat was a little ashamed to realise she didn't miss her mother. Not in the way one should miss a parent. It was almost a relief not to have to deal with her mum's issues. The drinking. The depression. The never knowing what she would find at the end of the phone when she called. Morose moods. Mania. Mayhem. 'Thanks,' she said.

Cricket came bolting back out, did a couple of crazy spins and yapped three times at Kat. Miranda gave a light laugh. 'Looks like he's taken a bit of a shine to you.'

Kat smiled back. 'It's mutual.'

Miranda went off to join Jaz in getting dinner organised, so Kat took the opportunity to speak to Flynn in private. As soon as she entered the sitting room, his gaze met hers from where he was sitting on one of the plush sofas. 'So, you've met half of the family.'

She sliced him a glare. 'Feeling pretty proud of yourself, are you?'

He gave her a lazy smile. 'It had to happen sooner or later. Miranda and Jaz are like sisters to me. I've known them since they were in pigtails.'

Kat folded her arms. 'I suppose you'll have Richard just drop in next. If he does, I'm out of here. I don't care how rudely I come across.'

He studied her for a beat. 'I didn't know the girls were going to show up. I was speaking to Jake about a legal matter and I mentioned I'd broken my foot. He must've told Jaz and she told Miranda. They arrived just as I was getting out of the cab.'

Kat kept her gaze trained on his. 'Why did you tell them you tripped down the stairs?'

He gave a light shrug. 'I didn't want to make things awkward for you.'

'I thought the whole point of this exercise was to make things as awkward for me as possible.'

'The girls are keen to have an amicable relationship with you. Why would I go and tell them you maimed me? They might never speak to you again.'

'*Maimed* you?' It's three tiny little bones, for God's sake. Talk about a drama queen.'

'It hurts like the very devil.'

She went over and whipped the glass of Scotch out of his hand. 'That is not allowed. You heard what Jaz said. You shouldn't mix alcohol with prescription drugs.'

His lazy smile made the base of her spine shiver. 'I'm having a hot fantasy of you dressed in a nurse's uniform. Ever played one?'

'Will you *stop* it? The girls will hear.'

His dark eyes glinted. 'We can't have the girls thinking anything untoward is going on between us, now can we, Miss Winwood?'

She gave him a look that would have withered marble. 'As if I would stoop so low.'

Jaz came breezing in with a tray loaded with nibbles. She looked at Kat's glowering expression and then at Flynn, who was smiling like a cat with an empty bowl and whiskers dripping with cream.

Jaz gave him a cheeky grin. 'That Carlyon charm not quite hitting the mark, eh, Flynn?'

'You know me,' he said. 'The harder I have to work for something the more I enjoy the victory.'

'Looks like you might've met your match,' Jaz said. 'I haven't seen you so hooked on anyone since Claire.'

The atmosphere changed as if an unpinned grenade had been dropped.

Flynn's expression turned to stone, his eyes to flint and the atmosphere to freezing. Kat glanced at Jaz but if Jaz was put off by Flynn's demeanour she showed no sign of it.

Miranda came in at that point and gauged the stiff little tableau with a worried flicker of her gaze. 'What's going on?'

'I mentioned the C word.' Jaz took one of the

nibbles and crunched into it loudly. Defiantly loudly. He-should-get-over-himself loudly.

Flynn reached for his crutches. 'Excuse me, but I'm going to give dinner a miss.'

Kat stood back as he limped past without once glancing her way. But she didn't have to see his face to know it was as tense as the muscles in his back and shoulders. *Interesting.* She waited until he was well out of earshot. 'Who is Claire?'

Jaz handed her a platter of nibbles. 'His ex-fiancée. Eleven years ago, to be precise. He's been gun-shy about commitment ever since.'

'Jaz, you really shouldn't have said anything,' Miranda said. 'You know how he hates anyone reminding him.'

Jaz shrugged off her friend's reproach. 'So, what's he got to be so uptight about? I've got three ex-fiancés and you don't see me getting upset if anyone mentions them by name.' She gave a twinkling grin and reached for her drink. 'Anyway, I've just about forgotten their names now I've got Jake.'

'How long was Flynn engaged?' Kat asked.

'Only a few weeks,' Miranda said. 'But he must

have really loved her. He was devastated when she broke it off. He wouldn't talk about it, not for ages. I don't think he even told Julius or Jake all the ins and outs of what went wrong. He can be pretty tight-lipped at times.'

'I think it comes from him being adopted,' Jaz said, and at Miranda's cautionary look added, 'What?'

'You know he doesn't like everyone knowing about that,' Miranda said.

'It's all right,' Kat said. 'He told me he was adopted.'

Miranda's eyes went wide. Not saucer wide. Satellite-dish wide. 'Did he?'

Jaz gave Miranda another little conspiratorial nudge. 'See? What did I tell you? He's got it bad.'

'Have you met his family?' Kat asked, trying to ignore the traitorous little flutter of excitement Jaz's comments evoked. 'I mean, his adoptive one?'

Jaz bent down to give Cricket a snippet of smoked salmon. 'I met his mother last year when I was in Manchester for a bridal show. She was nice in a standoffish way. I got the feeling she didn't really get Flynn. I think he intimidates her with his intelligence. Not that it's his fault he's so smart and has done so well for himself. He's always been driven and superfocused.'

'He said he has no interest in meeting his biological parents,' Kat said. 'Do you know why?'

'I think a lot of men who've been adopted are like that,' Miranda said. 'I guess they find it hard to understand what it's like for a woman to have to make that impossibly difficult decision to relinquish a baby.'

'Maybe he'll tell you since you're getting on so well,' Jaz said to Kat with a spark in her gaze.

Kat gave her a speaking look. 'Don't hold your breath.'

The girls left after an hour of eating and chatting on lighter topics. Kat found it a surreal experience to be on such familiar terms with the two young women she'd spent the last three and a half months actively avoiding. She even felt a little sad once they'd left. Their tight unit reminded her of all she had missed out on as a child. She hadn't had close friends growing up, or at least not as close as Jaz and Miranda were. She had moved around too much when her mother had changed jobs or relationships. It had been hard to create a bond with friends when in the back of her mind she knew it wouldn't be long before she would be taken away to some other place where she would have to start all over again. Her friend Maddie was the only exception, but even then they had met as adults, when Kat had visited Maddie's beauty salon when she'd first moved to London, and their friendship had grown from there.

She wondered if she would see Miranda or Jaz again or if by seeing them it would bring her into contact with her father. She wasn't ready to meet Richard Ravensdale. She didn't think she would ever be ready. How could she stand in front of a man who had wished her existence away?

But the thought of meeting her half-brothers was tempting. Miranda had spoken so highly of them. What would it be like to have twin older brothers to watch out for her? To have a family who included her in their lives?

Who actually *wanted* her in their lives?

* * *

Kat put some food on a tray and carried it upstairs with Cricket at her heels. Flynn's door was closed so she had to put the tray on a hall table outside before she could knock. 'Flynn? Are you awake? I brought you some dinner.'

There was no answer so she opened the door. Flynn was lying on his back with his foot elevated, his eyes closed, but she could tell he wasn't asleep. There was too much tension in his body. She could see it in the terrain of his face: the twin lines running down either side of his mouth, the groove between his brows, the in and out flare of his nostrils, as if he was carefully measuring each breath. Was it his foot giving him grief or had Jaz's mention of his ex-fiancée done that to him? Eleven years was a long time to be bitter over a relationship break-up. She tried to imagine him as a man in love. He didn't seem the type to let his emotions rule his head. He was charming and laid-back, but always in control. Or was his bitterness anchored in the fact that Claire had been the one to walk out? Some men found rejection hard to take. Perhaps his being adopted had made him even more sensitive to it.

Kat came and sat on the edge of the bed feeling a bit like a kitten approaching a lion. 'So, I take it Jaz struck a raw nerve?'

'Not raw. Dead and buried.' His tone was flat, emotionless, but she could hear a speed hump of hurt. 'I hate having it exhumed. It stinks.'

Kat hadn't realised how close her hand was to his where it was resting on the bed. If she moved her pinkie a few millimetres it would come into contact with his. Something shifted in her belly at the thought of his darkly tanned skin touching hers. 'She's quite a personality, isn't she?'

He grunted something unintelligible.

'I liked Miranda too,' Kat said. 'A lot. I didn't expect to but she's nothing like I expected. I thought she'd hate me, but she made me feel like she really wants us to have a connection.'

'She's a sweetheart. Leandro's a lucky man.'

Kat looked at their hands again. Watched as the distance between their fingers got smaller. Was she moving her finger or was he moving his? 'Were you in love with her?'

'Who?'

'Claire.'

His lips folded inward like he was filtering his response. Blocking it. Banning it. The silence boomed with the beats of the muscle flicking in his jaw. In. Out. In. Out.

'If you'd rather not talk about it...' Kat left the words hanging. Dangling like a dare.

His gaze hit hers. Hard. Two-can-play-at-that-game hard. 'Do you want to talk about your affair with a married man?'

Shame turned Kat's stomach sour and made her face burn. 'You *know* about that?'

'Men like Charles Longmore can't help boasting about bedding a celebrity.'

Panic took an ice-pick to her spine and a sledgehammer to her heart. If Flynn knew then who else knew? Would her shame be splashed on every tabloid? Everyone would blame her. They always did. The Other Woman always got the blame. No one ever blamed the philandering husband. Kat would be cast in the role of home wrecker and there would be no way to defend herself. 'Oh no...'

'It's all right.' Flynn's voice had a reassuring steadiness to it. 'He and I have come to an understanding.'

Kat swallowed back bile, her hammering heart going back to where it belonged in her chest. 'How do you know him?'

'Mutual acquaintance.'

She looked down at her clenched hands. 'I didn't know he was married. He lied to me. Lie after lie after lie. I broke it off as soon as I found out. The worst thing was I'd always been so annoyed with my mother for getting involved with married men. I feel like *such* a hypocrite.'

Flynn put his hand over her white-knuckled ones and gave them a light squeeze. 'Don't be so hard on yourself. He was a jerk. A cheat. No one will believe him anyway.'

'Why do you say that?'

'You're way out of his league.'

Kat cocked her head at him. 'Is that a compliment, Mr Carlyon?'

His smile tugged on her resolve like a child pulling at its mother's skirt. 'Yes, Miss Winwood. It is.'

Another small silence ticked past.

Kat relaxed her hands and smoothed them against her bent thighs. 'I guess I should let you rest...'

'I wasn't in love with Claire.'

Kat wondered why that should make her feel such an odd sense of relief. It wasn't as if she was worried about whether his emotions had taken a battering. Why should she care if he'd had his heart banged up?

*You do care. You like him.*

*No, I don't. Well...maybe a little...but only because he was so good about that creep Charles.*

'Claire thought she was pregnant,' Flynn said. 'I wanted to do the right thing by her and our child.'

'At least you didn't pay her to have an abortion.'

He gave her a fleeting half-smile before his expression went back to neutral. 'It was way earlier than I'd planned to settle down, but I thought it would work out if we both were committed to doing the best thing for the baby. But she found out a couple of days later it was a false alarm. She ended our relationship then and there.'

Kat searched his inscrutable face. What emotions was he screening from view? How had he felt at having the future he had planned with Claire cut so abruptly? Or had he been privately relieved he was off the hook, so to speak? Many young men would be terrified at the thought of fatherhood being thrust upon them before they were ready. 'You weren't relieved?'

He gave a soft laugh. 'No. Maybe later, when I'd got over myself a bit. But not then.'

'Why was doing the right thing by her and the baby so important to you? Because you were adopted?'

He met her gaze in a lock that made something in her chest ping. 'I wasn't a straightforward adoption.'

'What do you mean?'

Kat saw his deepening frown, the slow blink, the tight swallow, the shadow of something pass through his gaze. Several somethings. It looked like he was shuffling through his thoughts, deciding whether he should reveal what he had stored inside the filing system of his mind.

'I was a foundling,' he finally said. 'An abandoned infant with no name, no registration of birth or any other details pinning me to another soul on this planet. All I had was the ratty old bunny rug I was wrapped in and a soiled cloth nappy. And the worst case of nappy rash the authorities had ever seen.'

Kat stared at him in shock, her heart jolting at the thought of him as a tiny baby, suffering, abandoned, alone. 'Oh dear, that's so sad. Didn't anyone ever come forward?'

'Nope.' The way he said the word made it sound as if he had long ago given up hope. Maybe he hadn't had it in the first place.

Kat covered his hand with hers. Not that she did a great job of covering much of it, given her hand was so much smaller. He turned her hand over and entwined his fingers with hers. The heat from his hand warmed her body from her fingertips to her toes. 'I can't imagine what that must be like for you,' she said. 'Not knowing. Never knowing.'

His thumb moved back and forth against the fleshy base of hers. 'Maybe it's better not to know, or so I keep telling myself. I can't see myself turning up any famous actors as my parents.'

Kat pulled her hand out of his. 'I suppose you think I'm being petty about my father.'

'He's the only one you'll ever have.'

'He's not the one I want.'

'We don't get to choose.'

She got off the bed and stalked to the window, folding her arms across her body. 'I'm not ready.'

'That's another thing you might not have much choice over,' he said. 'What if you run in to him sometime?'

Kat swung back to face him with a look that would have curdled milk. 'You mean with another impromptu dinner party at your house?'

'I didn't engineer the girls turning up.'

'You engineered me house-sitting next door.'

'So?'

'So how can I trust you?'

He let out a long breath. 'The question is, can I trust you?'

Kat frowned. 'Why would you ask that?'

His gaze was direct. Don't-mess-with-me direct. 'I've told you stuff I've told no one. Not even the Ravensdales know I was abandoned as a baby. They only know I was adopted.'

Kat shifted her mouth from side to side, wondering if he regretted telling her. She seemed a strange ally for his secrets. She had made it clear she didn't like him and yet he had told her things he had told no one else. Or did he suspect she *did* like him? That she liked him more than she wanted to admit to herself? 'Why did you tell me?'

One side of his mouth lifted in a wry smile and he reached for his crutches to get off the bed. 'I have absolutely no idea. Maybe it's the painkillers and alcohol combination.'

Kat wondered if it was because he saw something in her that he saw in himself: the bone-deep sense of aloneness, of not belonging anywhere or to anyone. Of always having to rely on yourself with no one as backup. 'I won't tell anyone. You have my word.'

'And when you make a promise you keep it, right?'

She glanced at his slanted mouth. Right now she wished she had never made that crazy promise to her friend Maddie. Right now all she wanted to do was press her lips against his and taste the sensual heat of him, to feel the potency of him awakening every female pore of her body into an inferno of lust.

He came to stand in front of her but because he was on crutches his mouth was closer than normal. She could see every line and contour, the way the edges turned up at the corners, as if he was used to smiling far more than not. It impressed her that he was so positive in outlook, considering his tragic beginnings and the way his adoptive family held him at arm's length. Most people would be bitter and angry at the world. *A little like me.* So many people from difficult backgrounds became difficult people. The cycles of neglect and abuse often went on for generations.

But Flynn had made something of himself, refusing to let his tragic background stop him from achieving all he set out to achieve. He had qualities she couldn't help admiring. Most of the men she had been involved with had exploited her in some way. But Flynn hadn't sabotaged her fledging relationship with Miranda and Jaz, even though he'd had a perfect opportunity.

Why had he done that?

What did it mean?

Why was he treating her as if he had plans for building a future with her?

Kat looked into the dark-brown depths of his eyes, her stomach free-falling when they went to her mouth. He leaned one hand on his crutch and lifted the other to her face in a *fainéant* movement from the top of her cheekbone to just beside her mouth, his fingertip leaving a trail of fire against her skin. She sent her tongue out over her lips, swallowing deeply as she sensed him leaning closer. Her pelvis registered his proximity, her inner core contracting with a pulse of vicious need.

His mouth hovered above hers, his warm, faint-hint-of-whisky breath wafting over her tingling lips. His nose bumped against hers, a soft nudge that was powerfully, shamelessly, erotic. His stubble-shadowed skin grazed her cheek, sending her senses into a swishing, swirling tailspin. The tip of his tongue stroked the vermillion border of her bottom lip, a caress so intoxicating, so arousing, it nearly knocked her off her feet.

But somehow Kat managed to gather her scattered senses long enough to realise she had won a vital point against him. 'You kissed me.'

His eyes contained a dark glitter that put that point she'd scored in jeopardy. 'That's not a kiss.'

'You touched my lips with your tongue.'

'Nah-ah. I touched the edge of your lip.'

'You're taking hair splitting to a whole new level,' Kat said. 'You did so kiss me.'

His mouth lifted in that devilish smile that did so much lethal damage to her self-control. And her resolve...*wherever the hell it was*. 'That's not a kiss.' He leaned closer. 'But this is.'

# CHAPTER SEVEN

IN THE END, Kat wasn't entirely sure if he or she had closed that final distance. All she knew was as soon as Flynn's mouth came into contact with hers every thought of resisting him flew out of her head like bats out of a cave. His lips moved against hers with gentle pressure, not crushing, but cajoling hers into a passionate exchange that made every knob of her spine loosen. Her mouth flowered open beneath the first stroke of his tongue, the intimate invasion a toe-curling reminder of the act both their bodies craved—had craved from the moment they'd first met.

Was that not why it was so hard to step away and tell him to back off? Was that not why she had made that celibacy pact, because from the first moment she had laid eyes on him she had *wanted* him? She had recognised the danger he represented to her—the danger of being involved with someone where she wasn't the one in control.

Her body was dizzy with longing for more of his drugging kiss. Her tongue tangled with his in a heated duel; it was a combat of wills, a collision of personalities, a celebration of all that was physically arousing between a man and a woman. Her mouth was on fire with the potency of his, the assault on her senses unlike any other kiss she had received in the past.

For one thing, he wasn't holding her, on account of his crutches. It was only his mouth that was connected to her. His lips were fused to hers, drawing from her a response that was wild, hungry and desperately needy. Was it because she hadn't been kissed in weeks and weeks—months, even? Or was it because Flynn's kiss spoke to her on a level no one had ever been able to reach? She wanted to melt against his body but his crutches were an impediment. He was tilted towards her but if she pushed against him she was concerned he would fall. She wound her arms around his waist, her breasts coming into contact with the hard wall of his chest, but even that was enough to put him off-balance.

He lifted his mouth off hers and clutched at his crutches to rebalance himself. 'This isn't working quite the way it should.'

Kat lowered herself back on her heels, her hands falling away from his body, her cheeks hot as a bonfire. Two bonfires. Possibly three. What was she doing? Where was her self-control? Her resolve? *Where the heck was her flipping resolve?* 'I suppose you think I'll fall into bed with you now you've kissed me.'

His eyes were dark and glinting. Victory glinting. I-want-you-and-I-know-you-want-me glinting. 'You could fall or you could walk the couple of steps. I'd offer to carry you but I'm not sure I could pull it off with these sticks.'

'I'm not going to sleep with you.'

'But you want to.'

Kat laughed but even to her own ears it sounded fake. *So much for the actor's handbook.* She was going to have to brush up on the not-interested-in-you look.

She *was* interested in him.

He excited her. He challenged her. He thrilled her.

She had never met a more mesmerising man. Her senses were still reeling from having experienced the heart-stopping heat and passion of their first kiss—a kiss that had been months in the making. The chemistry between them had built each time they had been in contact. Every look, every bantering word exchanged, every locked gaze, had led to a kiss beyond anything she had experienced before.

What would happen if she allowed things to go further?

Making love with Flynn Carlyon would be dangerous. How could she keep her heart disengaged when he was already ambushing her with his wit, his humour, his intelligence, not to mention his Olympic-standard determination? He wanted her and wasn't afraid to let her know it. The knowledge of his desire for her spoke to her own desire for him like a secret code embedded in her body. She could feel the electrifying shockwave of longing every time he looked at her with that

smouldering gaze. The silent message he con-
veyed moved through her body, making her pulse
race and her heartbeat escalate. 'I'm not getting
involved with you.'

'Because I'm too close to your father?'

Kat knew it wasn't just because of her father.
It wasn't even because of her celibacy pact with
Maddie. It was because she knew getting involved with Flynn would not be a simple affair.
The way he made her feel was so different from
anyone else. She hadn't fallen in love with anyone before. But then she had never got to know
anyone so well before. She'd had infatuations and
mild crushes, but she hadn't learned anything
about them as people.

But with Flynn it was completely different.

She had got to know him over the last few
months, finding out more and more things
about who he was, what he wanted, what he
represented. The values he held. The information about his background was deeply personal
stuff and yet he had chosen to reveal it to her.
It made her feel as if their relationship was on
a completely different footing from any she'd

had before. No one had ever come close enough to make her want the fairytale. She had always been career focused, not marriage-and-family focused.

But Flynn made her *feel* stuff. Stuff she didn't want to feel. Not just a potent attraction but a sense of relating to someone who understood what it was like always to be on the outside.

But what did *he* want?

He was a commitment-phobe, or so Miranda and Jaz had intimated. Was he interested in her only so he could get her to Richard's party by fair means or foul? She was a task he had to accomplish, a box that had to be ticked.

Or did he want her because he too felt this powerful connection that pulled and tugged at every organ in her body?

Kat gave him a pointed look. '*Are* you close to my father? Are you close to anyone?'

The glint dulled in his eyes. 'Don't try and analyse me, Kat.' He turned away on his crutches to settle back in a sitting position on the bed.

'Why haven't you had a serious relationship since Claire?'

'Been there, done that, packed away the tuxedo.'

'So you're not interested in ever settling down?'

'Nope.' The word sounded like it was under-lined. In bold.

'Once bitten, twice shy?' Kat said. 'Seems a bit defeatist, if you ask me. What if you fall in love?'

'I won't.'

'Is that something you can control?'

'I've never met anyone I want to spend the rest of my life with.'

'But that could change,' Kat said. 'You could meet someone tomorrow who completely rocks your world.'

His eyes held hers for a beat. 'So could you.'

She looked away first, watching out of the cor-ner of her eye as he made his way back to the bed. He lay back on the pillows, propping his arms behind his head. 'Can you unzip my boot for me?'

Kat approached the bed with a scowl that would have sent a drill sergeant running for cover. 'Would you like me to bring your pipe and slip-pers while I'm at it?'

He smiled a breath-snatching smile. 'If I told

you what I'd like you to do you'd blush to the roots of your hair.'

She pressed her lips together, undid the zip on his leather boot and slipped it off his foot. His bandaged foot was swollen and there were purple and black streaks running between his toes. She touched her fingers to his foot to check for excessive heat. 'Do you need more painkillers?'

'No, I'm fine, but you can take the food away.' He closed his eyes as if signing out for the night. 'I'm not hungry.'

Kat hovered at the end of his bed. 'Are you sure you're okay?'

He opened one twinkling eye. 'A goodnight kiss wouldn't go astray.'

Her lips hadn't stopped tingling from the last one. She wasn't game to do a repeat. Her self-control was on a precarious knife-edge as it was. 'You don't give up easily, do you?'

His smile was one of those lazy, spine-melting ones. The ones that made her want to dive headfirst into his bed and crawl into his skin. 'We want the same thing,' he said. 'Sex without complications.'

'Sex is always complicated.'

'Maybe you haven't had the right partner.'

Kat put her hands on her hips. 'So you think you are?'

His eyes kindled. 'I'm damn sure of it.'

She tried to ignore the pulse of lust that throbbed in her core. Throbbed and ached. 'How can you be so confident?'

His eyes moved over her flushed features, lingering the longest on her mouth. 'One kiss told me all I needed to know. That's why you won't do it again, because you're frightened you won't be able to control yourself.'

'*Really?* Is that what you think?'

'Come here and prove me wrong.'

Kat knew she should resist his challenge but she wanted to prove it to herself as well as him. She would show him she could press her lips to his and feel nothing. No fireworks. No shooting stars. No fireballs of lust ripping through her body.

She stood next to him and lowered her mouth to his smiling one. It was the only point of contact, lips on lips. But he didn't respond. He didn't do anything to prolong the kiss. In fact, he didn't do anything but lie there like a mummified body.

Wasn't he *feeling* anything?

*Anything at all?*

She pressed her lips back down again, moving them against the firm warmth of his in a slow-moving caress. She couldn't remember a time when she had kissed a man with such concentrated intensity. It was as though all the nerve endings in her body had gathered in her lips, heightening their sensitivity. She sent out the tip of her tongue to trace the seam of his mouth, the touch slow, sensual and soft. She did it again, once, twice, and then the third time he gave a swift intake of breath and took control of the kiss. His arms came around her, bringing her down on the bed beside him, his mouth clamped to hers in a searing kiss, their tongues teasing and tangling, their lips sliding and sucking, their teeth nipping and tugging. She felt the full force of his arousal against her thigh, the potent power of it triggering her own intimate moisture.

He rolled her so she was half under him, his mouth still pressed hotly to hers. She swallowed a gasp as he slid one of his hands across her breast in a light skating touch that left her aching for more. She stroked his hair, his face, his back and shoulders as he plundered her mouth, inciting her desire to a level she had not thought possible. Never had desire rushed through her at such a breakneck pace. It was as if a drug had invaded her system, powering her up to do things she normally would never dream of doing. She reached for his belt and unhooked it, then went for his zipper. She wanted to feel the throb of him in her hand, to feel the desire he felt for her skin-on-skin.

He made a guttural sound when she got his zipper down, responded by slipping a warm, dry hand up under her sweater to cup her breast. Even though she was still wearing a bra her senses went wild. Off-the-scale wild. Scarily out-of-control wild. The promise of more was there in his hand as he cradled her. It was there in the roll of his thumb over her lace-covered nipple, making it go pebble-hard.

He left her mouth to bring his down to her breast, sucking on her through the lace, then when she thought she could stand it no longer he deftly unhooked her bra and drew on her with his warm, moist, tantalising mouth.

Kat reached for him with desperate fingers, peeling back the fabric of his underwear to access the satin-covered steel of his flesh. He made another deep sound of approval as she explored his length, concentrating on the blunt tip where his pre-ejaculate fluid had gathered.

His mouth left her breast to concentrate on the other one, subjecting it to the same delicious torture until she was writhing with longing beneath him. Such swift arousal was unusual for her. She wasn't used to her body aching with such urgent pressing need, as if she would die if he didn't follow through and complete their union. She could feel her clitoris stirring, swelling and aching for contact, for friction. The frustration of being so close and yet not close enough was making her resolve melt like a sugar cube dropped in a pot of hot tea.

*Who cared about the stupid celibacy pact?*

She wanted him. She wanted him with every

cell in her body. She wanted the release his kiss hinted at, the release his hard body promised.

Flynn's mouth came back to hers in another passionate onslaught that made her senses sing like a choral symphony. A thousand-member choral symphony. But just when she thought he would take it to the next level he drew back, breathing heavily but still in control. 'As much as I'd like to finish this, I'm going to call a halt.'

Kat called on every bit of acting expertise she possessed to look cool and composed when inside she was screaming, *Don't stop now!* 'Because you think I wasn't going to?'

He brushed a strand of hair off her face, his eyes holding hers in a lock that made her insides wobble like a jelly near a jackhammer. 'It's something else, isn't it? This thing we have going on.'

Kat edged out from under him and put some order to her clothes. 'There's no *thing* going on. We kissed and fooled around a bit, that's all.'

'I want you, Kat, but I'm prepared to wait until you're willing to admit you want me too. We do this as equals or not at all. Your choice.'

'What is it you want?' Kat said. 'A fling? A future? A one-off? Or is this just a ploy to butter me up so I agree to meet my father?'

'This is about us.' The deep, coming-from-beneath-the-floorboards pitch of his voice made her insides shiver. 'It's been about us from the first moment we met. That's why you were about to rip my clothes off just then and have your wicked way with me.'

Kat kept her gaze away from his unzipped trousers but it took a mammoth effort. Two mammoths and a couple of weightlifters thrown in. 'I have to go. I'll see you in the morning when I take Cricket out.'

'Do you want to meet for lunch tomorrow? I have a space between clients between one and two.'

'I'm working.'

'Then I'll have lunch at the café with you. You get a lunch break, don't you?'

'I'm not working at the café tomorrow,' Kat said. 'I have…an audition.'

Interest sharpened his gaze. 'What for?'

'Just a pantomime thing.'

'If you reached out to your father you'd be able to—'

'I do not need his help to get a job,' Kat said. 'If I can't get it on my own merit then I'll quit altogether.'

'Acting is in your blood,' Flynn said. 'You won't be happy unless you achieve what you've set out to achieve.'

Kat raised one of her brows. 'That sounds more like a description of you rather than me.'

'It's a description of both of us,' he said. 'Good luck tomorrow.' He gave her a wink. 'Break a leg. Or should I say, foot?'

Kat was on her way to the audition when she got a call from her friend Maddie. She was going to ignore it but she had already been a bit slack at responding to a couple of texts, which she knew would make her friend suspicious. 'Hi, Maddie.' She injected brightness into her tone. 'I've been meaning to call. Just been crazily busy, you know how it—'

'What's this I hear about you living next door to Flynn Carlyon?' Maddie said.

'Where did you hear that?'

'There's a photo of you on Twitter. You two are trending.'

'It's not what you think—'

'Have you broken the pact?' Maddie 's voice had a note of suspicion. A whole stave of suspicion.

'No-o-o-o.' Kat strung her answer out like she was stretching a piece of string. Or the truth.

'Have you kissed him?'

'I…erm…he kissed me.'

'Did you respond?'

What a question. What choice had she had? It had been the best kiss she'd ever experienced. Everything in her had responded—every cell, every pore, every atom. Every kiss henceforth would be measured against Flynn's searing sensuality and found lacking. 'I didn't let it go too far,' Kat said.

*He didn't let it go too far—not you.*

*I would have stopped eventually.*

*Like when? After he'd given you the big O?*

'How far?' Maddie said.

Far enough to want more. Far enough for Kat's body to be aching with the need to feel his arms around her, his mouth pressed to hers, his hard body doing all the things to hers she craved. Like the big O. 'Where was the photo taken?' she asked.

'Aha! Diversionary tactics. You are *so* going to lose this bet.'

'Kissing is allowed,' Kat said. 'We agreed on that.'

'There's kissing and there's kissing,' Maddie said. 'Which side does Flynn fall on?'

'You don't want to know.'

Maddie laughed. 'I knew you'd be the first to break. You just can't help yourself, can you? A handsome man takes a shine to you and you fall madly in love.'

'I'm not in love with Flynn Carlyon,' Kat said. 'I just have a body-crush on him.'

'He is rather gorgeous,' Maddie said. 'Even on crutches.'

'You've seen him on crutches?'

'That's the photo on Twitter I was telling you about,' Maddie said. 'You were standing outside his house with him with the snow falling down around you with a weird little dog at your feet.

It looked like a shot for a Hollywood romantic comedy.'

There was nothing comedic about their relationship. It was turning into high drama. How could she possibly avoid the temptation of him when she was forced to spend time with him? Time she *looked forward to* in spite of her misgivings about him and his connection with her father. 'I ran over his foot.'

'On purpose?'

'By accident. You know what I'm like at reverse parking,' Kat said. 'He was standing behind the car and—never mind. It's a long story. I'm helping him walk his dog and run errands for him while he's out of action.'

'Ah, but is he out of action in the bedroom?' There was a teasing lilt in Maddie 's voice. 'I can't see a pair of crutches getting in the way of what Flynn Carlyon wants.'

'What about you?' Kat was desperate to steer the conversation away from her nemesis. 'Have you fallen off the wagon?'

'No,' Maddie said. 'Not even tempted by anyone.'

'Sure?'

There was a tiny silence.

'Well, I do have to visit my great-grandfather this weekend for his birthday and you know who will be there.'

'Why will Byron be there?' Kat asked. 'You guys broke up months ago.'

'I know, but Gramps's dementia has worsened since his stroke,' Maddie said. 'He thinks we're still together and Mum thinks it will stress him out if we tell him any different. It's just a weekend. I can handle that. Anyway, good luck with the audition. Call me as soon as you hear, okay? And remember—I knew you before you were famous.'

# CHAPTER EIGHT

KAT WAS THE last person to audition, which meant by the time her name was called her stomach had grown teeth and they were gnawing all the way to her backbone. The director asked her to take position, but instead of feeling the buzz of being onstage she felt sick. What if she blew it? What if she made an idiot of herself? Who was she kidding? She was an amateur. She hadn't been to a performing arts school. She had rehearsed in front of a mirror, not an acting coach. All she was good for was toilet-paper ads. She was rubbish at acting.

She was rubbish, period.

'Ready when you are, Miss McTaggart.'

It took Kat a moment to realise the director was speaking to her. She had used her grandparents' surname instead of her own. 'Erm…right.' She stepped into position. The contents of her stomach curdled and began to crawl towards her wind-pipe. Sweat broke out on her brow. Her throat felt like someone had put a choke collar around it. A studded one, around the wrong way. The stage lights were making her eyes water. Or maybe it was because she felt ridiculously out of her depth. The spotlight was focused on her but she felt like it was shining on all of her faults. The irregular-ities of her features, the figure she wished was fuller in some places and more toned in others. The hair she hadn't had time or money to have professionally styled. The supermarket brand of make-up she'd used instead of a designer brand.

The stalls were in darkness but Kat noticed a woman sitting at the back of the theatre. The woman was dressed in nondescript clothes but she had an aura about her that suggested she wasn't one of the theatre or ancillary staff. She looked vaguely familiar but because the lights were off in the stalls it was hard to make out any distinguishing features.

'Is there a problem, Miss McTaggart?' The di-rector's voice contained a thread of impatience. A steel-cable thread.

'Sorry.' Kat wriggled her shoulders to shake off the tension. 'I'm just getting into character.'

'Would you like a bone to chew on?' the woman at the back of the theatre asked in a tone dripping with sarcasm. Not dripping—flooding.

Kat bristled like a cat, which wasn't all that helpful, given she was supposed to be a dog. She took a deep breath and channelled her angst at the woman into her performance, using it to galvanise her into the performance of her life. She *became* Sylvia. She used every bit of Cricket's quirkiness she had born witness to: his pleading looks, his energy, his over-the-top excitement and his frantic rear-end wagging and wriggling. She felt so authentic in the scene she wished she had a tail when it was over so she could wag it.

'Thanks, Kathy,' the director said. 'I'll let you know what we decide in a day or two.'

The woman at the back of the theatre rose from the chair she was sitting on. 'I've already decided,' she said in an accent that this time Kat recognised as none other than Elisabetta Albertini's. 'I want her. She was by far the best.'

Kat's eyes widened as Elisabetta came out of

the low light of the stalls towards the stage. Her dream felt like it was balanced on a high wire without a safety net. As soon as Elisabetta recognised her it would plummet to the cold, hard floor of reality. There was no way Elisabetta would want to star alongside her husband's love child. No way in the world. It wouldn't matter how brilliant a job she had done of the audition. It would be better to get in first to save everyone from embarrassment. 'Erm…my name isn't really Kathy McTaggart,' she said. 'My name is—'

'Katherine Winwood,' Elisabetta said. 'Yes, I know.'

Kat fought hard not to be intimated by that cold, dark-brown, assessing stare. Was Elisabetta searching for her husband in Kat's features? As much as Kat knew it must be galling for Elisabetta to face the living, breathing evidence of her husband's betrayal, she still wished she could be accepted at face value, for herself, not for the trouble she had inadvertently caused. 'I really want the part but if you'd rather not work with me then—'

'Didn't you just hear me say I wanted you?' Elisabetta gave an imperious arch of her brow.

'Yes, but I thought since—'

'I want you in that part,' Elisabetta said. 'Fix it, will you, Leon?' she said to the director. She turned back to Kat. 'Rehearsals start on Monday. Be on time.'

Kat had trouble keeping her jaw off the floor as Elisabetta walked out with regal poise. Had that just happened? Had Elisabetta Albertini just insisted *she* get the part?

But why?

Was it because of her talent or was this some sort of publicity stunt? She hadn't shown a skerrick of talent until Elisabetta had insulted her. How could she know for sure what Elisabetta's motivations were? What if Elisabetta wanted to sabotage her career? What better way to get back at her husband Richard than by publicly humiliating his love child onstage?

'Looks like you got the part,' Leon said. 'Congratulations.'

'Thanks.' Kat mentally chewed at her lip. What if this was not about her acting merit? What if this was all about revenge? Wasn't it the director's or casting agent's decision as to who got the part? Or had Elisabetta insisted on choosing whom she would front up with onstage? She had a reputation as a diva. And she certainly had the star power to call the shots. No one would ever employ Kat again if this turned out to be a stitch-up.

Why had Elisabetta chosen her other than to use it as an opportunity to get back at her?

The self-doubts sat like anvils on her shoulders. Her dream of being onstage was turning into a nightmare. The whole world would watch Elisabetta cut her down. It was risky but the determined streak in Kat's personality thrived on the chance to prove to Elisabetta and to everybody she was made of stronger mettle. She would not be rattled or thrown off her game by a vindictive attempt to ruin her one chance at stardom.

'Ruby the costume designer will measure you in Dressing Room B,' Leon said. 'I'll email the contract to your agent.'

Flynn was sitting on his sofa with his foot up after work, reading through a client's brief, when he got a call from Jake Ravensdale. 'Jaz tells me you're done like a dinner over Kat Winwood,' Jake said. 'Want to double up at my stag night? Half the cost, twice the fun.'

Flynn pushed the papers off his knee and Cricket promptly rested his furry chin on them, looking up at him with hopeful eyes. He reached out, absently stroked the little dog's ears and was rewarded with a blissful puppy sigh. 'My plan is to get her to your father's party, not into church.'

'Come on, man, you know Dad only wants her there to placate his fans,' Jake said. 'He doesn't care a jot about her. Miranda and Jaz were quite taken with her. Do you reckon she'll agree to meet Julius and me sometime, like at your wedding?'

'Very funny,' Flynn said. 'But I want Kat to meet your father. I think it would be good for her. It will give her some closure. Even if she tells him to his face what she thinks of him.'

'That's going to be fun to watch,' Jake said. 'So, how's the foot? Must be tricky sweeping her off her feet when you're on crutches.'

Flynn eyed his bandaged foot with a scowl. 'You can say that again.'

'So is she The One?' Jake said.

Flynn let out a swift curse. 'What is it with you Ravensdales? You all get hitched within a month or two of each other and then try and recruit everyone else in your circle to do the bloody same.'

'Just want you to be happy, mate.' Jake adopted a serious tone for once. 'You're so jaded about settling down because of all those dirty divorces you handle. But life is short. Before you know it, you'll be staring down the barrel of retirement. Is that all you want to show for your life? Work, work and more work?'

'Listen,' Flynn said. 'I'm glad you and Jaz got your stuff sorted. You're a great couple. Perfect for each other in every way. But leave me to my miserable life with work, work and more work, okay? I'm fine with it.'

*Was he fine with it?* Flynn thought once he had signed off on the call a moment or two later. Ever since Kat had come into his life he felt…different. Like the colours in his day were brighter, which was weird, since it was one of the bleakest, greyest winters on record. He felt sharper within himself, more switched on. More focused. He enjoyed life more, felt more potent, even though he hadn't had sex in... When *had* he last had sex? He screwed up his face as he tried to recall his last relationship, not that it had been a relationship in any sense of the word. He had only slept with the woman a couple of times way back in September at a law conference in Newcastle before he'd lost interest.

*September?* Had it really been that long? He had been so focused on Kat Winwood since early October that no one else had taken his eye. He couldn't even bear the thought of trying it on with anyone else. Who would match her for intelligence and feistiness? The chemistry between them was phenomenal. He had only to look at her and he wanted her. But it was more than a physical lust. Over the last few months he had got to know her. Getting to know a partner other than in the biblical sense was not usually high on his priorities.

But with Kat he felt he understood her. He could read her mood, even when she did her best to hide her emotions. Underneath all that feistiness and shtick was a sensitive girl who hadn't had it easy.

And Cricket loved her, which was the best litmus test of all.

There was that word 'love' he usually steered clear of. Love was an emotion that had let him down from as young as he could remember. Sometimes he wondered if his abandonment as a baby had done something to his brain, changed its architecture or something, making him distrustful of any bonds no matter how genuine they appeared.

But he didn't want to be tied down with the responsibility of a relationship… *Did he?* The thought kept returning like a tongue to an irritable tooth. Before he'd met Kat he had been perfectly at peace with his decision to keep his relationships casual. He knew marriage was something that worked well for some people. Even his adopted parents, for all their other faults, were committed to each other and there was every indication they would remain that way for the rest of their lives.

But he saw plenty of other marriages. Horrible marriages. Bitter marriages. Marriages where the warring parties tore each other to shreds and where children were used as pawns and payback.

He wanted no part of it.

Cricket whined and wriggled up closer to put his head on Flynn's knee with a look of complete and utter devotion, as if to say, 'I love you and will never let you down.' Flynn ruffled the dog's ears again. 'I love you too, buddy,' he said, a little shocked to find his voice catching slightly over the words.

Kat let herself into Flynn's house to save him the trouble of having to answer the door on crutches. She was later than usual, as the audition had run over time, plus she'd had to feed Monty and convince him to sit on her knee long enough for the Carstairs family to be assured their beloved pet was being looked after properly. Thankfully Monty hadn't scratched her this time, but he'd coughed up a fur ball in her bedroom, which seemed a little too deliberate for her liking.

Cricket came like a NASA rocket out of the sitting room, his toenails scrabbling on the marbled hallway, his little body skidding like a drunken skater on loose ice skates. She bent down and he leapt into her arms and gave her face a virtual baptism. 'Yes, you crazy little excuse for a dog,' she said, laughing. 'I love you to bits, too.'

She looked up to see Flynn had limped to the doorway after all. 'Sorry I'm so late,' she said. 'I had to feed Monty and quickly Skype the Carstairses before I came over.'

He glanced at her hands. 'No scratches? Things must be looking up between you two.'

Kat gave him a rueful smile. 'We're getting there, slowly but surely.'

There was an enigmatic twinkle in his eyes. 'Not a bad way to do things.'

She reached for Cricket's lead. 'I'll just take Cricket out now.'

'Don't worry about taking him out tonight,' Flynn said. 'It's foul outside. How did your audition go?'

She put Cricket's lead back on the hallstand. 'I got it…'

'You don't sound too excited.'

Kat let her shoulders down on a sigh and faced him. 'I'm not sure I got it for the right reasons.'

'Did the director recognise you?'

She didn't bother hiding her worry. She had a feeling he knew it anyway by the way he was looking at her. Softly. Understandingly. 'No, but Elisabetta Albertini did. She's playing the role of Kate in *Sylvia*. I didn't know that otherwise I would've thought twice about auditioning. She was sitting at the back of the theatre and, after insulting me when I took a bit of time getting over my nerves, she insisted the part was given to me.'

'You must've done a good job. She's picky about who she works with.'

'I can't help feeling I'm being set up,' Kat said. 'I looked like such an amateur up there. I was quaking in my shoes. I've never felt so nervous in my life. What if she only wants me in that part so she can make a fool of me?'

His gaze lost none of its softness; if anything it got softer. Tender, almost. 'You need to work on your confidence, sweetheart. She'll eat you alive if you show you're intimidated by her.'

Kat's heart was still skipping over the word 'sweetheart.' Lots of men used terms of endearment and they usually meant nothing. Sweet nothing. But somehow the way Flynn said it gave it weight. Substance. A foundation she could stand on while the rest of the world trembled with uncertainty. 'Do you think she'd do it? Ruin opening night to get back at me?'

'Do you want me to have a chat with her?'

She gave him a horrified look. 'No!'

'You're not really frightened of her, are you?'

Kat tossed her hair back off her shoulders—a gesture of bravado straight out of the actor's handbook. She just wished she felt the indifference she was portraying. 'Of course not.'

'How about we go out to dinner tonight?'

Kat frowned. 'Dinner?'

'To celebrate you getting the part.'

She chewed at her lip. 'I don't know...'

'Ouch.'

Kat looked up at him in concern. 'Is your foot okay?'

He grinned at her. 'That was my ego, not my

foot. How many times does a guy have to beg a girl to go out to dinner with him?'

She looked at him narrowly. 'Just dinner?'

'I'd offer to take you dancing, but can you see me burning up the dance floor on these sticks?'

Kat's conscience and willpower went into battle again.

*Dinner will be fine.*

*You think?*

*Of course it will. We'll have a drink, eat a meal. Go home. Simple.*

*You'll sip champagne while gazing into his dreamboat eyes and start planning how many of his babies you'll have.*

*I will not. Anyway, he's not the settling down type.*

*But you are.*

*Am not. I want a career. Stardom. My name up in lights.*

*And then what?*

*And then I'll be happy.*

*Yeah?*

Kat forced a smile. 'I'm not much of a dancer

myself. I've never been able to get through a waltz without pulping my partner's toes.'

He smiled with his eyes, making her stomach free-fall. 'Sounds like you just haven't found the right partner.'

The restaurant Flynn took her to in a cab was owned by one of his clients. They were given the best table in the house in a romantic corner that gave them privacy from the other diners. Flynn ordered champagne and, once it was poured, raised his glass to hers in a toast. 'To your brilliant career.'

Kat took a sip of the delicious bubbles whilst looking into his eyes that were dark as pitch, yet soft and melting. How on earth was she going to stop herself from falling in love with him when he looked at her like that?

*You're well on your way.*

*No, I'm not. I'm just aware it could be a danger, that's all.*

*Stop looking at his mouth. Dead giveaway.*

Kat put her glass down and shifted in her seat,

keeping her gaze trained on the cleft in his chin. 'So…how was your day?'

'Look at me, Kat.'

She looked. Felt her heart kick at the way his knowing smile curved up the corners of his mouth. The mouth that had kissed hers—kissed it and made it hungry for more. So hungry it was all she could do to keep herself on her side of the table. Her knees bumped against his, sending a shockwave of awareness through her body, concentrating in the heated core of her womanhood. Warmth flooded her, need oozing, the ache of lust building with every beat of the silence as his gaze tethered hers. 'Wh-what?'

'You're nervous.'

'I'm not.'

'When was the last time you went out to dinner with a guy?'

Kat let out a long sigh and looked at the salt-and-pepper shakers on the crisp snow-white tablecloth. 'September last year. Charles the creep. I was so ashamed I was physically sick when I found out he had a wife and three little kids, one of them only a few weeks old.' She brought her gaze back up to his. 'How can men do that to their wives?'

Flynn made a twisting movement with his mouth. 'There are some prize jerks out there, that's for sure. I come across them all the time in my line of work. You'd be shocked at how many men try and wriggle out of paying for their kids once their relationship with their mother is over.'

Kat fiddled with the stem of her glass. 'I just hate how I didn't see it. That I didn't see *through* him. How could I have got it so wrong?'

He placed his hand over her restive one, the warmth and steadiness of it moving through her entire body like a soothing wave of a calming, cleansing drug. 'You did the right thing by getting out of it as soon as you found out. But I can see how it would make you cautious.'

She looked at their entwined hands, hers so light against the tan of his. 'I've always prided myself that I'm nothing like my mother. She was hopeless at reading men. She was in and out of dysfunctional relationships all through my childhood. I never knew who would be there when I got home from school. Sometimes it was so scary.

I couldn't understand why she couldn't see the innate badness in some of the men she brought home. *I* could see it and I was just a kid.'

Flynn's expression was gravely serious. 'Were you ever in danger? Did any of your mother's men friends hurt or interfere with you?'

Kat pulled her hand out of his light hold on the pretence of brushing back a wayward strand of hair. She didn't trust herself to touch him for too long. His touch made her body hunger for him. Hunger and ache. 'A couple of times I had to fight off some unwanted attention, mostly when I was a teenager. It was worse when Mum was drinking. She just didn't pick up on stuff. I couldn't talk to her about it, as she would get angry and blame me for being too mouthy or whatever.'

His frown formed a bridge between his eyes. 'But in spite of it all you still loved her?'

She gave him a crooked smile. 'Yeah, well, that's what kids do, isn't it? Their survival depends on it—loving their caregivers. Not that she was great at caregiving or anything. But, yes, I loved her.'

'Is that why you don't want kids?' he said after

a moment. 'Are you worried you won't do a good job of mothering your own kids?'

Kat picked up her glass for something to do with her hands. 'I guess on some level… But I really want to achieve what I set out to achieve first. If I get tied down with kids and marriage, I'll never reach my goal.'

'What if fame isn't everything you think it will be?'

'It's not just the fame,' Kat said. 'I've wanted to act for as long as I can remember. I know I won't be satisfied until I exhaust every opportunity to make it onstage. It's not like I want to prove it to anyone else. I need to prove it to myself.'

'It's a tough life, working for weeks and then nothing for months,' Flynn said. 'There are good years and bad years. Plays fold without notice or run for season after season until you're bored out of your brain for the want of something fresh and more challenging. Then there are the great reviews and the awful ones. You have to have a tough skin.'

She met his dark gaze across the table. 'And you don't think I have one?'

'Underneath that tough exterior is a girl with a soft heart. I see it. Cricket sees it. Miranda and Jaz saw it. Probably Elisabetta saw it, which is why you're feeling so threatened by her.'

Kat had always prided herself on the impenetrable armour she wore around her heart. But in his presence she could feel it falling away, piece by piece, like a glacier fracturing. He seemed to understand her in a way no one had ever done before. It was hard to keep her defences up when he was so strong and supportive, so intuitive and accepting of her. 'Do you think I should meet Julius and Jake?'

'They wouldn't want you to do anything you're not comfortable with. But they're on your team, Kat. We all are.'

'Apart from Elisabetta,' she said with a downturn of her mouth.

He reached across the table and covered her hand with his. 'Let your talent do the talking. You have no reason to doubt yourself.'

Kat stroked her fingers over the flesh of his thumb, feeling a rush of lava-hot heat go from his body to hers. His eyes held hers in a lock that said all that needed to be said. The message was erotic, exciting, thrilling. Urgent. The need that pulsed between them made her inner core vibrate with a longing no amount of celibacy pacts could withstand.

Resisting him any longer was pointless. They had been moving towards this moment from the first time they'd locked gazes. She wanted him and couldn't bear prolonging the agony. She could no longer find any reason not to explore the chemistry between them. So what if he wasn't the settling down type? She wasn't ready for the white picket fence and cottage flowers either. All she wanted was to feel his arms around her, to feel alive in the way a man can make a woman feel when they both like and respect each other. She couldn't think of a man she liked and respected more than Flynn.

Maybe that was what she had been doing all wrong with dating up to this point. She had dated men who weren't her equal intellectually, not strong enough to stand up to her and *for* her. They had only been interested in her body, not her mind, her emotions, her ambitions, her drives and aspirations.

'If we were to get involved…hypothetically speaking…' Kat chanced a quick glance at him. 'What would you want out of it?'

His thumb found the nerve-rich centre of her palm and began stroking a mesmerising caress across the sensitive flesh. 'You mean apart from sex?'

Kat's belly quivered at his touch, at his words, at his smouldering-coals look. 'I mean…would we be having a fling or be in a…a relationship?'

'You said "relationship" like it was a prison sentence.'

'Yes, well, some of mine have been a bit like that.'

His stroking continued, stoking a fire within her body she could feel deep and throbbing in her core. 'What about your celibacy pact?'

'I've proven my point to my friend. Besides, I think she's going to break it herself this weekend. She's going to be within arm's reach of her ex. Always a dangerous prospect for her.'

'Whose idea was the pact?'

'Mine mostly,' Kat said. 'I just got tired of getting involved with men who were shallow and not interested in me as a person. Or ones who told blatant lies.'

'Well, if it's any comfort, I'm not married, haven't been and was only engaged for forty-eight hours eleven years ago,' Flynn said. 'Every other relationship—and I use that term loosely—has been temporary.'

Kat stroked her fingertip over the blunt end of his thumb, watching as his dark ink-like pupils flared with molten heat. Even the candle on the table flickered, as if it was tired of competing with the flame of attraction glowing between them. 'So…if we get involved what will we call it?'

His mouth slanted in that spine-tingling manner. 'How about a flingsationship?'

She gave him an answering smile. 'I've never heard of one of those. What does it involve?'

He winked at her. 'Let's go back to my place and I'll show you.'

# CHAPTER NINE

IN THE CAB on the way back to Flynn's house Kat could feel desire flooding every inch of her body like the wash of a warm tide. Flynn was holding her hand against the strong muscles of his thigh, an intimate anchoring of her to him that made her fingers itch to creep closer to the hot, hard, tempting heat of him. He glanced down at her with a teasing glint in his eyes. 'Don't even think about it,' he said in a sexy undertone. 'There are security cameras.'

Touching him was all she could think about. Touching him, stroking him with her fingers, licking him with her tongue. Tasting him. She communicated it with her gaze, a kind of visual foreplay that made his pupils flare and his hand tighten over hers. 'Just wait till I get you alone,' she said.

'You'll have to be gentle with me. I've got fractures.'

Kat bit her lip as she glanced at his bandaged foot. 'Will it make it…?'

'Awkward but not impossible,' he said, holding her gaze.

She saw the hunger there, the need, the longing. *For her.* Had any of her partners looked at her like that? As if she was the only woman in the world he wanted to make love to? 'When was the last time you…?' She left the question hanging open.

'September.'

Kat raised her brows. 'Why so long between drinks?'

He kept his eyes trained on hers, the heat in his fuelling the fire already raging in her flesh. 'Because when I set my mind to something I don't allow distractions to take my focus off my goal.'

Kat licked her lips with a quick dart of her tongue. 'How long were you prepared to wait?'

'However long it took.'

'What if I didn't play ball, so to speak?'

'I knew from the moment we met you would.'

It wasn't just hubris on his part. Kat had known it too. Deep in her body she had known he was the one man she would not be able to resist. She reached up with her hand and stroked his lean and tanned cheek, his light stubble catching on her fingers. 'I hope I'll be worth the wait.'

Something softened in his expression. 'Is that a lack of confidence I hear again?'

Kat puffed out a little sigh. 'It's easier for guys. Simpler. For women it's a little more complicated...or at least, it is for me.'

He cupped her cheek with his warm hand, his eyes holding hers in an intimate lock. 'I'll make it good for you. I promise.'

'Even with crutches?'

The look in his eyes made every knob of her spine shudder in anticipation. 'Count on it, baby.'

Keeping Cricket out of the bedroom proved to be more of a challenge for Flynn than getting her into it, Kat thought wryly as she listened to the little dog whining and scratching on the other side of the door. 'Do you think he'll settle down?'

Flynn reached up to loosen his tie. 'I'm not

making love to you with a dog breathing down my neck.'

'But he sounds so miserable.'

'He'll get over it.' He tossed the tie to one side. 'Now, come here so I can undress you.'

She looked at him balanced awkwardly on his crutches. 'Maybe we should switch it around. I'll undress you.'

His dark eyes gleamed. 'Be my guest.'

Kat made him sit on the bed and knelt down between his spread thighs to unbutton his shirt. She peeled it off his broad shoulders, leaning into him to press kisses to his warm, tanned, muscular flesh, from the base of his neck to the tightly whorled cave of his bellybutton.

She heard him snatch in a breath as her tongue circled his navel, but he put his hands on her shoulders to stall her from going any lower. 'That's not the way I plan to do this,' he said. 'You're pleasure is my priority. My goal.'

Kat shivered at the steely intent in his gaze. 'What do you want me to do?'

'Take your clothes off. Slowly.'

Kat got to her feet, balancing on one foot and

then the other as she removed her heels. She slid her tights down from beneath her simple black dress, letting them fall in a twisted heap on the floor next to her shoes, all the while holding that dark-as-night, hungry gaze. She reached behind her back to pull down the zipper on her dress, letting the fabric shimmy down her body before it too landed in a puddle at her feet. She lowered one bra strap and then the other, her breasts still cupped in their black lace. She unhooked the back of her bra and watched as his eyes devoured their shape. She had body issues, just like any other young woman her age, but somehow standing in front of him in nothing but her knickers made her feel as if she was the most beautifully proportioned woman he had ever seen.

Cricket gave a piteous whine from the other side of the door, scratching at the woodwork as if he was determined to dig his way through to his beloved master.

Flynn muttered a curse. 'I can't freaking believe this.'

Kat laughed at the agitated look on his face. 'Let him in. I don't mind. Really.'

He mock-glowered at her. 'I'm not having a threesome with a dog.'

She moved closer to the bed, hooking one finger under the edge of her knickers. 'Have you ever had one?'

He frowned. 'A threesome? No. Not my thing at all. You?'

Kat shook her head. 'A guy I was dating asked me to a while back but I refused. Needless to say, that relationship didn't last long.'

'Nice to know I'm not the only conservative lover around.'

She arched a brow and eased her knickers a little further down. 'How conservative are you?'

His smile made her insides shift and shudder in delight. 'Come over here and I'll show you.'

Kat stepped out of her knickers and moved within touching distance, her breath leaving her chest in a little gasp as his hands settled on her hips. She stood between his legs, her hands resting on his shoulders, her heartbeat tripping like a foot missing a step when his mouth came to her breast. He glided his lips along the sensitive flesh, his tongue passing over her budded nipple in a teasing, barely touching stroke that made every nerve ending beg and plead for more. He suckled on her gently before switching to her other breast, torturing her spinning senses with the promise of fulfilment.

There was a building storm in her body—a storm of need that refused to be ignored. She could feel the tension in her lower body, the delicious pulse and contraction of her womanhood, the deep ache that begged to be assuaged.

He guided her to lie down with him on the bed, somehow removing his trousers and underwear before he came down beside her, his damaged foot off to one side out of harm's way. He stroked the seam of her body with a slow-moving fingertip, his touch like fire against bone-dry tinder. He explored her more intimately, sliding one and then two fingers into the secret cavern of her body, coming back to the swollen bud of her clitoris, massaging it with such deft skill she came apart within seconds. The sensations rippled through her body, fanning out from her core to all of her limbs, even to her very fingertips, in wave after wave of spine-tingling pleasure.

He planted a warm hand on her belly. 'But wait. There's more.'

Kat sucked in a breath as he brought his mouth to her. The feel of his lips and tongue on her most intimate flesh made her whole body shake and shudder. The earth-shattering orgasm thundered through her body, hurtling her into a vortex unlike anything she had experienced before. She was breathless when it was over, stunned that her body could respond with such violent fervour.

Flynn gently lifted a strand of hair away from her mouth and tucked it behind her ear. 'Was that as good as it looked?'

Kat touched his mouth with a fingertip. 'You know it was.'

He captured her finger and pressed a soft kiss to her fingertip. 'You could've been pretending.'

'I'm not *that* good an actor.'

He kissed her fingertip again. 'Repeat after me: I. Am. A. Brilliant. Actor.'

Kat tried to pull her hand away but he held firm. 'This is silly...'

'Say it, sweetheart.' His eyes wouldn't let hers go. 'Say it for me.'

She took a breath and released it in a whoosh. 'I. Am. A. Brilliant. Actor.'

He smiled and inched up her chin. 'I want you.'

Kat drew in another sharp breath as his eyes seared hers. She could feel the swollen heat of him against her thigh and reached down to take him in her hand. She moved her hand up and down his shaft, watching as he fought for control with every movement of her hand.

'Hold that thought,' he said and rolled away to retrieve a condom from the bedside drawer.

*See? He's done this a thousand times.*

*So?*

*You're just another notch on his bedpost.*

*Firstly, he doesn't have a bedpost—he has a bedhead. Secondly, he's waited months for me. That makes it different.*

*What makes you think you're so special?*

*He likes me. And I like him.*

*You're falling in love with him.*

*I'm doing no such thing.*

Flynn paused once the condom was in place. 'Are you okay?'

Kat quickly rearranged her features. 'Sure.'

A tiny frown appeared between his eyes. 'We don't have to continue this if you'd rather not.'

She smoothed out the crease of his frown. 'I guess being a lawyer and all you'd be pretty pedantic about consent.'

'It's not about me being a lawyer. It's about me being a man who respects a woman's right to say no at any stage of the encounter.'

*You are so going to fall in love with this guy.*

Kat ignored the debate with her conscience to gaze into his dark eyes. 'I want you. I really, truly want you.'

His mouth came down to hers in a slow burn of a kiss, stoking the fire of her need until her entire body was shaking with it. She whimpered, she begged, she clawed at his back and urged him to put her out of her misery, but still he took his time pleasuring her with his mouth, with his tongue, playing, flirting and teasing hers.

'Don't be so impatient,' he said against her lips.

'Aren't you…you know…?'

His erection moved against her folds, potent, thick and heavy with desire. 'I am, but I want you to be ready for me.'

*I was ready for you the first time I set eyes on you*, Kat wanted to say out loud. But instead she used her body to do the talking, pushing herself against his swollen heat, her breath catching as he entered her slickly in one deep thrust that made every hair on her scalp tingle and twirl. He groaned as he surged again, the rocking movement of his body triggering powerful sensations in her core. She was close but not quite close enough. But, as if he could read her every need, he reached down between their entwined bodies and found the throbbing heart of her desire. His fingers worked their magic and suddenly she was flying, spinning, rolling over and over, losing track of anything but the explosive release pulsing through her entire body.

Flynn followed with a series of thrusts that signalled his own release. Kat felt the tension of him just before he pitched into the abyss, heard the guttural groan, felt the hot breeze of his expelled breath against her neck. She felt him relax against her when it was over, his arms still holding her as if he never wanted to let her go.

She tiptoed her fingers up and down the musculature of his back, exploring every knob of his spine, from between his shoulder blades to the base just above his taut buttocks. She felt his skin quiver like a horse shaking off an insect. 'Am I tickling you?' she said.

He leaned on his elbows to look at her. 'You have beautiful hands. But then everything about you is beautiful.'

Kat traced the outline of his mouth with her fingertip. 'This is kind of weird...'

'What is?'

'Me being in bed with you.'

'Doesn't feel weird to me. It feels amazing.'

She looked into his coal-black gaze. Had he felt anything like the cataclysmic release she had felt? 'Better than usual?'

His expression was closed for a nanosecond, as if he had retreated to some place in his mind where no one else was allowed access. But then he smiled a lopsided smile. 'Fishing for compliments, Miss Winwood?'

Kat pulled at her lower lip with her teeth. 'Will you tell Jaz and Miranda and the twins about us?'

His eyes moved between each of hers, as if he

too were searching for something she was try-ing to conceal. 'Would it bother you if they found out?'

She thought about it for a moment. 'Not re-ally…as long as they know this isn't heading any-where serious.'

Something about his expression looked tight. Pulled back. 'Wedding fever might've hit the Ravensdales but it's not going to hit me.'

Kat studied the taut line of his mouth for a mo-ment. 'I would've thought you'd be the first per-son to want to settle down and have a family.'

'Why's that?'

'Because you didn't have one growing—'

'I did have one.' He rolled away from her to dispose of the condom. 'I still have one.'

'But you're not close to any of them.'

'So?' He threw her a glance. 'Lots of people aren't close to their families. It doesn't mean they don't love them.'

Kat pulled her knees up to her chest and wrapped her arms around her legs. 'You love them?'

He let out an impatient breath. 'Of course I do. They raised me, educated me, provided for me.'

'Do you ever tell them you love them?'

He reached for his trousers, sitting on the bed with his back to her and pulled them on. 'We're not that sort of family.'

Kat watched as he got awkwardly to his feet to shrug on his shirt. 'Are you angry with me?'

He turned to look at her. 'Why do you think that?'

'Because you're getting dressed. It's like you're putting up a barrier.'

He drew in a long breath and then released it in a measured stream. 'It's late. I thought you'd want to go back next door to your own bed.'

*He's dismissing you. He's done the deed, now he wants you gone.*

*No, he's not. He's protecting himself. I've touched a nerve.*

Kat unfolded her legs and got off the bed. She didn't reach for her clothes but went over to where he was balanced on his crutches with his shirt hanging open. She slid a hand over the taut muscles of his chest, right up to the back of his neck to bring his head down towards hers. 'Do you really want me to go back next door?' she whispered against his mouth.

'Not yet,' he said and covered her mouth with his.

# CHAPTER TEN

FLYNN WOKE SOMETIME during the night to realise Kat was still in bed beside him. It wasn't that he didn't have the occasional sleepover but he was choosy about who stayed and who didn't. He had wanted Kat to stay. Had wanted it so much it spooked him. He kept telling himself it was okay; she wanted what he wanted—a fling-sationship—something between a fling and a relationship. It could last days, weeks or months and he was fine with that.

He looked at her sleeping beside him, her hair in a tangled mess across the pillow, her soft mouth settled in a half-smile as if she was dreaming about something pleasant. She gave a tiny murmur and nestled a little closer. It was as if she had sensed there was someone in the bed beside her and couldn't bear not to be touching them. He shivered as her arms and legs wrapped around his, her head burying against his chest as she gave a kittenish purr of satisfaction.

He found himself stroking the back of her head while he listened to the sound of her breathing, feeling each soft breath waft over his skin like a caress. One of her hands slipped down between their bodies, her fingers finding him as hard as stone.

She opened her eyes and looked up at him with a sultry smile. 'You're up already?'

Flynn shuddered as her hand tightened around him. 'Been up a while, actually.'

She sat up and pushed her hair back off her face, her beautiful breasts drawing his gaze like an industrial-strength magnet. He touched each one with his hand, cupping them, stroking them, watching as she expressed her pleasure with little sighs and moans. He leaned forward to take her nipple in his mouth, rolling his tongue over and around it, drawing on it with gentle pressure. Her hands came down to grasp his head, her fingers digging into his scalp as if to anchor herself against the powerful sensations his touch evoked.

He moved his mouth to her other nipple, then

to the underside of her breast, licking the sensitive flesh with his tongue until she pulled him away to look at him with eyes bright with desire.

She pushed him back down on the bed and straddled him, taking care not to bump his bandaged foot. Her hair half-covered her breast like she was a mermaid, which somehow was even more sexy than straight-out nakedness. He slid his hands up from her hips to her waist, his erection pressed up against her naturally separated folds. He could feel her wet heat, the temptation of her making his body hum with overwhelming longing to thrust in without protection.

But that was a line he wouldn't cross.

'Want to put a condom on for me?' he asked, nodding to the bedside drawer where he kept them.

She reached over, the lithe stretch of her body making his all the more frantic with excitement. She was slim and yet femininely rounded in all the right places. She undid the packet with her teeth as she held his gaze with the sensuous heat of hers. Then with torturous slowness she applied it to him, stroking it down his length, securing it in place with a couple of massaging strokes that nearly blew the top of his head off.

Then, when he thought he could take no more, she gave him a look from beneath her half-mast lashes and shimmied down his body so her mouth was within reach of his erection. 'I thought you were a conservative lover,' he said in a strangled voice.

She gave him a naughty girl look and got down to business. He took as much as he could before he pulled her away with a gentle but firm hand fisted in her hair. 'Enough,' he said. 'I won't be able to pleasure you.'

'We can take turns, can't we?'

Flynn stroked his hands up and down the silk of her arms. Her cheeks were rosy, her mouth wet from where she had sucked on him, her eyes sparkling with sexual excitement. 'I want to watch you come,' he said.

She looked momentarily uncertain. 'You mean while I'm on top like this?'

'If you're comfortable doing it that way.'

She came back over him and positioned herself so he could enter her, guiding him in with her hand. He felt the tight grip of her body, the slick heat drawing him in until he was mad with the need to let fly. He let her control the depth by holding her by the hips, thrusting up to meet her downward movements. The pleasure built to a crescendo, and for the first time since he'd been a teenager he wasn't sure he could hold on to his control.

He watched as her orgasm played out over her face, felt it in her body where it rippled and con-tracted around his. She was gasping, crying, whimpering, shaking and shuddering all at once, her head, with her wild hair, thrown back as she gave a primal sound that made him feel more of a man than he had ever felt before.

His own release was just as earth-shattering. It rocketed through him, leaving him breathless and boneless once it was over.

Kat slumped over him with her head nestled against his neck, her hair splayed across his chest in a silky wave. He stroked her slim back in long, gentle strokes, loving the feel of her satin-smooth skin against his palm.

His mind began to drift... What would it be

like to lie with her like this for morning after morning? To wake and see her lying beside him? To see her gorgeous face smile at him as if he was the only person in the world she wanted to wake to? To see her face at the beginning and at the end of each day? And not just her face but the faces of the children they could make together— a girl and a boy, or two girls or two boys. They could even foster or adopt. Make some kid's life a blessing instead of a curse.

Flynn snapped the lid down on his thoughts like someone shutting a Jack-in-the-box. Why did he have these thoughts around Kat of all people? She wasn't interested in settling down any more than he was. She was happy with a temporary relationship because she wanted to focus on her career.

She was young, eleven years younger than him. He had never had a lover that much younger. But she was far more mature than some of his previous partners who had been similar in age to him. He liked her sense of humour, her intelligence and her determination to succeed. He even liked the fact she was standing up to Richard Ravensdale. So many women in her shoes would have milked the situation for all it was worth. Milked it and made butter, yoghurt and custard out of it. But she had stood her ground. Refused to be bought. Refusing to be manipulated into doing anything she didn't believe was right for her.

Flynn wanted her at that party but not just to please Richard. He wanted her to feel connected to her siblings. To feel a part of the family, because he knew it would be good for her. She had no one in the world now her mother was dead. It would give her a safe haven to have older half-brothers and a half-sister to turn to. Even Jaz with her runaway tongue would be good for her. It would give Kat a community of love that appeared to have been sadly lacking in her childhood.

'I'd better get back to check on Monty,' she said into the silence.

Flynn stroked his hand up to the nape of her neck, her hair tickling the back of his hand where it was resting against it. 'He'll be fine. Cats are pretty self-sufficient.'

She lifted her head to look at him. 'Are you sure you want me to stay the rest of the night?'

He brought his hand round to cup her face. 'Isn't that what people who are having a fling-sationship do?'

'I wouldn't know, as this is my first.'

'Mine too,' he said and brought her head back down to his chest.

Kat woke to the feel of someone licking her face but when she opened her eyes it wasn't Flynn but Cricket. 'Eeeww!' She laughed and pushed him away.

Flynn came in on his crutches, showered and dressed for work. 'I would've brought you breakfast in bed but I haven't figured out how to do that whilst on crutches.'

'It's the thought that counts,' Kat said, getting out of the bed, picking up Flynn's shirt from the night before and slipping it on. She could smell him on the fabric, but then she could smell him on herself. Something shifted in her belly at the memory of all they had shared the night before. It wasn't just the physicality of sex, the mind-

blowing release or the sensual touches and ca-
resses. It was the sense of having drawn closer
to him than to any other person. She wondered
if he felt the same.

'I have an early meeting with a client,' he said.
'Will you be okay to take Cricket out?'

'Sure,' Kat said. 'I'm using him as research. I
think that's why I nailed the audition.'

Flynn smiled crookedly. 'Good to know he's
come in useful. Last night I was ready to drive
him to the dog's home.'

'You would never do that. You love him and
he loves you.'

His eyes moved away from hers and he picked
up something from the top of a chest of drawers.
'Dinner tonight?'

'I'll cook something for us here,' Kat said.

He turned to look at her. 'Sure you want to go
to that much trouble?'

'It was part of the deal, wasn't it?'

A small frown pleated his brow. 'I wouldn't
have held you to it. I could've found someone
else to walk Cricket, and I can afford to eat out
or have it delivered to me.'

'So why did you insist I do it?'

His expression had a hint of ruefulness to it. As if she had uncovered something about him he hadn't expected. 'I wanted to spend time with you. To get to know you.'

A warm glow spread through her. 'Do you spend time getting to know all of your lovers?'

'Occasionally.'

Somehow his answer disappointed her. She wanted to be the only one he took the time to get to know. She wanted to feel as special to him as he felt to her.

*See? What did I tell you? You're falling for him.*

*I'm not in love with him.*

*Not yet, but it won't be long.*

Flynn came over to her and eased up her chin so her eyes couldn't escape his. 'Where did you go just then?'

'Go?'

'In your mind,' he said. 'Every now and again you get this faraway look in your eyes, as if you're thinking about something.'

Kat pulled out a relaxed smile from her actor's handbook. 'I was thinking about tonight's menu.'

His eyes did that back-and-forth thing between each of hers. Left eye. Right eye. Left eye. Right eye. Then he looked at her mouth, making her belly turn over. 'Am I on it?' he said.

She stepped up on tiptoe and pressed a kiss to his mouth. 'You're the main course.'

Flynn came back home after a long day at work to find his house filled with delicious home-cooking smells. Cricket bounded up to him, spinning in circles in unmitigated excitement. The sense of home, of security, of belonging, was like a warm blanket on a cold winter's night. It settled around his shoulders, wrapping him in a cloak of contentment unlike anything he had felt before, if ever.

Kat came out of the kitchen. 'How was your day?'

'Long and tiring.'

'Dinner won't be long. I just have to carve the roast.'

'You cooked a roast?'

Her face fell. 'You don't like roasts?'

He brushed his fingers down her cheek. 'Love them.'

Her smile lit up her face. It was like sunshine after a month of cloudy weather. 'Go and put your feet up and I'll fix you a drink.'

'I feel like I've stepped into a nineteen-fifties time warp,' Flynn said. 'By the way, the apron looks great on you.'

She looked at him with a pursed mouth. 'I'm not going to ask you who wore it before me.'

'No one,' he said. 'It was a present from Jake a couple of birthdays back. He likes to joke around.'

'When is your birthday?'

'May. I don't know the exact date but apparently it's anywhere between the tenth and fifteenth.'

'Taurus,' she said, nodding. 'That makes sense.'

'Stubborn as a bull?' Flynn said. 'Yeah, that's me.'

She chewed at her lip for a moment. 'Is it weird not knowing the exact day you were born?'

'Birthdays aren't that important to me.' He had made them unimportant. He no longer ruminated over which day, hour, minute he was born and to whom. Well, not often.

'I guess you already know when my birthday is,' she said with a little frown. 'It seems like the whole world knows I was born two months after Miranda.'

He touched her face again. 'Any more thoughts about meeting Richard?'

She pulled away as if his fingers had burned her. 'No.'

'What about Julius and Jake? Would you be prepared to meet them?'

'Maybe.'

*That was a win if nothing else.* But the clock was ticking on that party date and he wanted her there. Everyone was expecting him to pull this off. She didn't have to stay long, just meet her father and get out of there, if that was what she wanted. 'I'll organise something when Julius and Holly come over from Argentina. They'll arrive a few days before Richard's party. Jake might catch up with you sooner but it'd be nice if you met them together.'

'Whatever.'

He brushed his thumb over her pouting mouth. 'They're good people, Kat. Don't put them in the same class as your father. He's in a class all of his own.'

She stretched her lips into a smile that didn't show her teeth. 'I'll get that drink for you.'

When Kat brought in a glass of wine to Flynn he was sitting with his feet up, Cricket curled up by his side. He was checking something on his phone but put it down when he saw her. He smiled as she handed him the glass. 'It's going to be tough going back to microwave meals.'

'Can't you cook?'

'I can but I don't always bother. Too much fuss for one person.'

'I know,' Kat said. 'I'm a bit the same.'

He patted the seat beside him on the other side of where Cricket was lying. 'Got a minute?'

'Sure.'

She sat down and he put his arm around her shoulders to draw her closer. 'I've been thinking about your job at the café,' he said. 'It's going to be tough getting to and from rehearsals.'

'I can manage.'

A little silence passed.

'What if I were to pay you?'

Kat swung her gaze to his. 'For what?'

He gave a little roll of his eyes. 'Not *that*. For helping me around the house. Walking Cricket and so on.'

She didn't have to think about it. Her pride wouldn't allow her to accept money off him or any man. Not unless she was officially employed, as in a proper job. 'No. Absolutely not.'

'But what if your shift runs overtime or you have a clash?'

'I'll cut back my hours,' Kat said. 'I'll swap shifts. I'll *make* it work.'

He let out a breath that had a hint of frustration to it. 'It's just money, Kat. I have plenty of it.'

'That's not the point.' She sprang up off the sofa and folded her arms as tight as a steel band across her body.

'What about if I gave you an interest-free loan?'

She gave him a wintry look. 'I'm not a charity case.'

He studied her for a beat. 'Oh, I get it. You

don't want to be beholden to me in case I turn the screws on you attending Richard's party.'

Kat pressed her lips together. 'It's not about that stupid party.'

'It's about your pride, isn't it?'

She didn't answer.

'Are you nervous about rehearsals on Monday?'

'A little.'

'Need any help with your lines?'

'I can manage.'

'Kat.' The way he said her name in that achingly gentle way brought her gaze back to his. 'You've been doing everything on your own for so long you've forgotten how to recognise a genuine desire to help,' he said. 'I want you to do well in that play.'

'Why?'

'Because I think you deserve this chance to show the world what you're made of.'

Kat released a breath she hadn't realised she'd been holding. 'Okay…if you don't mind. It would be good to run through my lines a few times.'

'I don't mind at all,' he said. 'I haven't seen the

play live but I've seen a couple of YouTube clips. We can work on it over the weekend.'

*This will be the clincher. Helping you with your lines. Sheesh... What's next? A wedding rehearsal?*

*What's wrong with helping me with my lines? Any friend would do that.*

*Friend? Is that what he is?*

*Well, he's not my enemy. Not now.*

Flynn tapped her on the end of her nose. 'You'd better not zone out like that onstage. Elisabetta will eat you for breakfast and spit out the leftovers.'

Kat blinked and pasted on a smile. 'I'll go and dish up. Don't move. I'll bring it in on a tray.'

The weekend passed so quickly it was Monday morning before Kat was ready. Not because she hadn't rehearsed her part in the play, but more because the time she'd spent with Flynn had been one of the happiest times of her life. He was such easy company, funny and relaxing to be around. He settled her nerves by getting her to go through her part numerous times. He had even gone to the trouble of downloading and printing the script so he could take Kate or Greg's part when needed.

Kat couldn't stop herself thinking what an amazing partner he would make. The way he supported her, encouraged her, challenged her to give more than she thought herself capable of giving. The evenings, they'd spent lingering over dinner and chatting over current affairs or life in general. His sharp mind kept her on her toes; he saw the flaw in any argument and had the mental flexibility to adopt any other position and argue from that corner with just as much skill as from the opinions he held himself.

But it was the nights in his arms she enjoyed the most. Not just the wonderful sex, which seemed to get better and better, but the closeness she felt to him. The sense of him understanding her on a level no one had taken the time or effort to do before.

Even the way he had rescheduled his first client so he could have breakfast with her on Monday morning made her realise how well he knew her. How had it happened? How had the man she had seen as her mortal enemy now become her biggest ally?

Kat could still taste his kiss when she walked through the back door of the theatre. Elisabetta was already there, talking with the director Leon and the other cast member playing Greg. There were stagehands about, as well as the costume designer called Ruby, whom Kat had met on the day of the audition.

It was clear from the moment they began the rehearsals that nothing Kat could do would please Elisabetta. She kept insisting on Kat redoing the scene, even though Leon had been reasonably happy with it. But apparently Elisabetta's demands overruled his opinion and he meekly allowed his biggest star to call the shots.

It was beyond exhausting but Kat hadn't fought this hard and for this long to be bullied by a woman who should have been professional enough to put personal issues aside for the sake of the theatre company and the sponsors. Kat called on every bit of determination she possessed to get through the session without biting back. She withstood the stinging criticism, she turned a deaf ear to the insults and she channelled her frustration into her acting.

'That's it for the day,' Leon finally announced. 'We're back on set at ten tomorrow. Well done, everyone.'

Elisabetta gave Kat a haughty look. 'You'll have to work harder. I'm not impressed by what I've seen so far.'

'You liked what I did in the audition,' Kat said. 'What's changed?'

Elisabetta's gaze could have stripped three decades of wallpaper off a wall. 'You think because you're his bastard child you can talk to me like that?'

Kat aligned her shoulders. Raised her chin. 'We're not on set now. I'll talk to you any way I like.'

Elisabetta's black eyes flashed with venom. 'He doesn't want you in his life, you know. He's only doing it for the publicity. To make his fans think he's a good man.'

'I know,' Kat said. 'That's why I don't want anything to do with him.'

Elisabetta's brows snapped together. 'You're not coming to his party?'

'Nope.'

Something hard in the older woman seemed to give way. It was visible in the small almost imperceptible sag of her shoulders, in the way her tautly held features ever so slightly relaxed. 'Why not?'

'Would you want to meet someone who paid to get rid of you?' Kat asked.

Elisabetta shifted her mouth back and forth as if she was shuffling words like cards inside her mouth. 'What's going on between you and Flynn Carlyon?'

'Nothing.'

Elisabetta smiled—the smile of a cat standing beside an empty birdcage. 'So he's managed to do it, then.'

'Do what?'

'Get you into his bed.'

Kat ground her back teeth together to try and control her temper. 'My private life is none of your business.'

'Don't get too cosy in his bed,' Elisabetta said.

'He won't offer you anything but a quick tumble when it suits him.'

'You know something, Ms Albertini?' Kat said. 'You're a wonderful actor, one of my all-time favourites. I've admired you from afar for as long as I can remember. But as a person? You're a bitter disappointment.'

At first Kat thought Elisabetta was going to slap her. The colour rose in the older woman's face in twin spots on her regal cheekbones, but then she tossed her glorious mane of salt-and-pepper hair back and laughed. Kat stood there waiting for it to end, sure another insult would follow and mentally preparing for it. Had she gone too far? Who in their right mind would insult one of London's most adored theatre actors? Was this the end of her career? Was it over before it had even begun?

An apology was forming on Kat's lips when Elisabetta stopped laughing and smiled at her instead. 'I like you, Kat Winwood,' she said. 'You've got G and D.'

Kat frowned in puzzlement. 'G and D?'

'Guts and determination,' Elisabetta said. 'Believe me, in this business you'll need it. I'll see you tomorrow. *Ciao*.' And with a wave of her hand and a swish of her plush velvet coat she disappeared through the stage curtains.

# CHAPTER ELEVEN

KAT HAD JUST returned from walking Cricket and was hanging up his lead when Flynn came in from work.

'How did today go?' he asked.

It occurred to her then how comforting it was to have someone to debrief with at the end of the day. Under normal circumstances she would have gone home to an empty bedsit. Sure, she could have called a friend or have a friend call her, but to have someone on site who was genuinely interested in her made her feel supported. Grounded. Safe. Protected. 'It was…interesting,' she said.

'Did Elisabetta behave herself?'

Kat took Flynn's coat from him and held it against her. She could easily have hung it up next to hers but she wanted to savour the warmth and smell of his body still trapped in the cashmere. 'She was hell on wheels during rehearsals, but

after everyone left we sort of came to an understanding.'

One of his dark brows lifted in an arc. 'That
sounds intriguing. Tell me what happened.'

Kat gave him a quick run-down on the conversation she'd had with Elisabetta. 'Mind you,' she
said. 'I wouldn't trust her, for all her charming
friendliness. She's like a chameleon. She changes
when it suits her.'

'That's why she has the reputation she has as
an actor,' Flynn said. 'She can morph into any
character she wants. But you did well to stand up
to her. Not many people do. They're too frightened of her celebrity to connect with the person
under the façade.'

Kat frowned. 'You think it's a façade? That
she's not like that normally? Bitchy and unfriendly to anyone she perceives as a threat?'

He leaned on one crutch as he brushed his bent
knuckles down her cheek. 'She's a bit like you.
You can be prickly and unfriendly until you establish trust. Maybe she recognised that same
quality in you.'

Kat turned and hung up his coat as she thought

about it. She straightened out the sleeves, dusted off an imaginary bit of lint from the back and turned to look at him again. 'What would you like for dinner?'

He was looking at her strangely. There was a slight frown between his eyes and his mouth had lost its easy smile. Then he did a slow blink and refocused. 'Sorry, did you say something?'

'I asked what you wanted for dinner,' Kat said. 'I didn't have time to pick anything up after the rehearsal, but I can go out now to the convenience store and—'

'No,' he said. 'This has gone on long enough. You don't need to wait on me hand and foot. I can order something in but only if you'll stay and share it with me.'

Would that be all that she was sharing? The thought of spending another night in his bed was tempting. More than tempting. But what if what Elisabetta had said was true? That he would only have her in his bed when it suited him? How long would it suit him? A week? A month? Until Richard's party was over?

*Why are you stressing about how long he wants*

*to sleep with you? It's a fling. They're not meant to last long.*

*I'm not stressing. I'm just wondering...*

*You're in too deep. You know you are. You've got feelings for him, deep, scary feelings that involve weddings and babies and a white picket fence.*

*I want a career first. It's all I've ever wanted.*

*So you keep saying.*

When the food arrived, Kat set it up in the dining room. Once they were both seated, Flynn raised his wine glass to hers. 'To the most beautiful new talent to hit London's West End.'

Kat gave a self-deprecating snort. 'I don't know about that. I've got so much to learn. It's a big step up from toilet-paper ads to playing Sylvia.'

'You got that part on your merit.'

She fingered the bottom of her glass. 'Did I? Or did Elisabetta choose me because she wants to get back at Richard by publicly humiliating me?'

He put his hand over hers, stilling its restless fidgeting. 'Look at me, Kat.' His eyes were dark and serious. 'Whatever her reasons were, you have to take control now. It's up to you. Actors have to deal with difficult casting arrangements all the time. Good actors don't bring their personal life to the stage. You have to be Sylvia on that stage, not Richard Ravensdale's love child. Understood?'

Kat let out a wobbly breath. 'You're right. You're so right.' She smiled. 'Thanks for the pep talk. If ever you get sick of practising law, you could be a life coach.'

His smile was rueful as he pulled his hand back from hers. 'Yeah, well, I'm good at sorting out other people's problems. It's different when it's closer to home.'

Kat searched his features for a beat. 'Is there something you're struggling with? Personally, I mean?'

His expression closed like curtains on a stage. 'No.'

His answer was too abrupt, too definite. Was he having second thoughts about their relationship? Did he want it to end sooner rather than later?

They ate in a companionable silence but Kat got the feeling he was mulling over something. Every time she glanced at him he was frowning.

It would relax whenever he caught her looking at him, and his smile would quickly replace it, but it only lifted half of his mouth.

Was his foot annoying him? Slowing him down at work? Her guilt over injuring him came back with a vengeance. Everything had changed between them once she had run over his foot. The dynamic of their relationship had changed. They had gone from enemies—at least on her part, that was—to lovers. Intimate partners in a fling-relationship that had a scarily loose time frame. It never used to bother her when she'd had temporary relationships in the past. It was just how things were. She had never felt a pressing ache in her chest at the thought of it ending. She had never envisaged a future together where she could have it all: the career, the loving and supportive husband, the kids, the house and the pets.

But now, after just one night sleeping in Flynn's bed, she realised how much she wanted to repeat it. To spend not just one night but many nights, all the nights that were allotted to her on this earth.

But what did he want? He had made it clear

he wasn't going to settle down. Even Elisabetta, who knew him well, had said the same.

'I bought you something today,' Flynn said into the silence.

Kat looked up in surprise. 'What? Why?'

He leaned back in his chair to reach for a small package on the sideboard she hadn't even noticed was there when she'd come in to set the table. He handed the package to her with an unreadable look. 'Actually, it's from Cricket,' he said. 'For taking him for all those walks.'

Kat unpeeled the satin ribbon and the paper to find a jewellery box from a well-known jeweller inside. Her heart flip-flopped. Jewellery? What sort of jewellery? She tentatively opened the box and found a beautiful tortured pearl on a delicately crafted white-gold chain. The pearl was irregular in shape but she knew from reading about them somewhere that each one was completely unique. Was he telling her something by this lovely gift? That he saw *her* as unique and special? She looked across at him. 'I don't know what to say...it's beautiful. But you shouldn't have bothered.'

'Cricket insisted,' Flynn said. 'Anyway, it's just a trinket.'

*A trinket?* Kat looked back at the gorgeous pearl. This was no throwaway trinket. This would have cost a packet. She had never been given jewellery as a gift before. In fact, as far as gifts went, she had received very few over the course of her twenty-three years. Her mother had never had enough spare cash for presents, and certainly none of Kat's past boyfriends had ever gifted her with anything—not so much as a bunch of flowers.

Kat leaned down to where Cricket was sitting at her feet waiting in hopeful enthusiasm for a titbit to be offered his way. 'Thank you, Cricket,' she said, ruffling his funny ears. 'You've made me feel very special. I'll treasure this for always.'

Cricket yapped as if he understood every word she said and then did one of his crazy little twirls.

'Mad dog,' Flynn said with a relaxed smile.

Kat met his gaze across the table again. 'I think he's the nicest dog I've ever met.'

*Are you talking about the dog or him?*
*The dog... Okay, both.*

*Sucker.*

Kat lifted the pearl and its chain out of the box and trailed it across her palm. 'Does Cricket buy all your lovers gifts?'

'You're the first because I've only had him since Christmas.'

She put the pearl back in its box and gently closed the lid. She was the first but wouldn't be the last. Why should that make her feel empty inside? As if a giant hole had been gouged in her stomach? 'What happened with your family that you ended up with Cricket?'

He picked up his wine glass and looked at the contents for a moment. 'There was a scene. There usually is at Christmas and birthdays—any occasion, really.'

'What happened?'

He took a slow breath in and released it in a whoosh. 'I didn't like the way my parents were treating Cricket. He's not the sort of dog you can lock outside, especially as they'd had him in the house since he was a puppy. We got into an argument and things escalated. My father's solution was to have Cricket euthanised.'

'Oh, no!'

'Oh, yes.' His look was grim. 'I left with Cricket and drove back here and had a perfectly lovely evening with the Carstairses and their kids. It was the best and worst Christmas, if you know what I mean.'

'I do,' Kat said. 'But how lovely that you've got him now. He adores you. It's like he's always been yours.'

That smile that made her insides melt was back. 'I haven't quite figured out the logistics of what to do with him when I go away on holidays or business,' he said. 'He doesn't strike me as the boarding kennel type.'

Kat reached down to scratch Cricket underneath his chin. 'Is your daddy calling you fussy, my sweet? You're not a fusspot, are you? You just love the comfort of home and I don't blame you one little bit.'

When she looked up again she caught Flynn looking at her with that odd look on his darkly handsome features. 'What's wrong?' she said. 'Why do you keep looking at me like that?'

His expression became blank. Unreadable. The

stage curtains not only pulled across but the lights turned out as well. 'How am I looking at you?'

'I don't know…as if you're uncertain about something…about me.'

He reached for the wine bottle to refresh their glasses. 'It's just work stuff playing on my mind. Big cases, big egos, big bucks involved.'

'I guess it's another good reason to avoid marriage,' Kat said. 'You see the other side of it—the dirty and bitter side. No wonder it puts you off.'

He put the wine bottle back in the silver cooler. 'Not all marriages end up in the divorce court. Some couples manage to last the distance, but you can never know if you and your partner are going to be the success story or the soul-destroying showdown.'

'True,' Kat said. 'But do you think it's more about good luck than good management?'

'A bit of both, probably,' he said. 'When I look at your brothers and sister and their partners, I can't imagine any of them ever wanting a divorce. But life can throw up some curve balls. Relationships can get knocked off course by all sorts of things. Bad health, financial stress, kids or the lack thereof, interfering relatives... The list is endless.'

'I guess communication is the key,' Kat said. 'Being able to talk about stuff—really talk, I mean. Not locking stuff away only for it to blow out in an argument when it's too late to fix it.'

He gave a wry smile. 'Listen to us. The experts on the institution both of us are actively avoiding.'

Kat smiled back but for some reason it felt false. 'Yeah, well, I didn't rule it out entirely. Just not right now.'

A long silence passed.

All Kat could hear was the ticking of the mantle clock in the sitting room next door.

'It's tough finding a partner once you're famous,' Flynn finally said. 'You can never know if people want you for you or for the social esteem it gives them to be associated with you. Both your brothers have struggled with that.'

'Has Miranda experienced it too?'

'She lost her boyfriend Mark when they were teenagers,' he said. 'Cancer. She hadn't dated since. She martyred herself until Leandro whisked her away to Nice to help him sort out his late father's estate. He's had a thing for her for ages. Everyone could see it except Miranda.'

Another silence ticked past.

'Does it happen to you?' Kat asked. 'The celebrity thing? I mean, you're so close to the Ravensdales. Do people use you to get to them?'

'Lovers, you mean?' he said. 'Occasionally, I guess. It doesn't really bother me, to be perfectly honest.'

'Because you only want them for sex?'

He looked at her for a beat or two. 'Putting it baldly, yes.'

*Was that all he wanted from her?* Their relationship was based on the physical chemistry they had, not on anything else. No lasting bond was being formed. No future path was being laid out. No plans were being made for continuing their relationship indefinitely. 'I guess I should count myself privileged you want me for other things as well,' she said, and held up her hand to tick off a list. 'Dog walking, cooking, running errands, scintillating conversation.'

His smile was a little twisted. 'I want you for lots of reasons.'

Her insides slipped sideways at his deep and husky tone. But common sense raised a red flag. 'You want me to go to Richard's party,' Kat said. 'Be honest. That's your primary goal. It has been from day one.'

'I'm not denying I want you there,' he said. 'But it's no longer my primary goal.'

She moistened her suddenly dry mouth. 'What is?'

His eyes smouldered as they held hers. 'Why don't we clear away here and I'll show you?'

Flynn woke from a disturbing dream later that night. It took him a moment to realise it had only been a dream. His heart was pounding, his skin was clammy and his pulse was racing like he'd had four energy drinks back to back. He had dreamt he was left alone on an island in the middle of the ocean. There was no power. No lights. No food. No shelter. No way of contacting anyone. A cruise ship was in the distance but it was too far for him to swim. There were sharks in the water. Menacing dorsal fins everywhere, circling the island. Every escape route was seething and swirling and swishing with danger.

He turned his head expecting to see Kat beside him in the bed but the space where she had been earlier was empty...well, apart from Cricket, of course. 'What are you doing in here?' he said. 'You're supposed to be sleeping in your basket downstairs.'

Cricket sank his undershot chin even lower onto his paws, his eyes taking on a beseeching look that would make anyone with half a heart think twice about removing him.

*But that was the trouble.* Flynn had more heart than he wanted right now. It was taking up more and more room in his chest, making him feel things he didn't want to feel. He couldn't explain why suddenly everything had changed when for so long he had been perfectly happy with his life. Seeing Kat arrive home earlier that evening had shown him what his life could be like if they were a couple. Not just dating or having a fling, but a committed couple.

He had been excited all day at the thought of

coming home. The thought of sharing a meal with her, talking to her, watching her with Cricket, making love to her, had distracted him all day. He had bought her that pearl in his lunch hour. A completely spontaneous thing he still couldn't explain. He had walked past that jeweller's hundreds if not thousands of times and never once had he looked at the display in the window. But that day he had felt compelled not only to look but to go inside. He had seen the pearl and instantly known it was perfect for Kat. It was unique and beautiful, just as she was.

He tossed the bedcovers aside and reached for his crutches beside the bed. He was completely over his foot. It wasn't so much the pain now but the inconvenience. He was tired of how it slowed him down.

Where was Kat? Had she gone back next door? He made his awkward way downstairs and saw that her coat was no longer hung up next to his. Her hat and gloves were not on the hall table. A cavern of emptiness spread in his chest like a flesh-eating stain.

He was alone.

\* \* \*

Kat knew Flynn was in a foul mood as soon as she arrived the next morning. She had left his bed the night before because he'd seemed restless while he slept. She'd assumed his foot was giving him trouble so she'd left so he could have the bed to himself without having to worry about her bumping him during the night.

There were other reasons she had left. One big reason, actually. Not that she wanted to examine it too closely.

He was in the kitchen stirring a cup of coffee, which seemed a little pointless, as he didn't take milk or sugar. His back was turned towards her and even though he was wearing a business shirt and trousers she could see the tension in his body. She could even sense it in the air, crackling like static. Even Cricket was acting a little subdued. He wasn't bouncing around and twirling in excitement but had a baleful look on his funny little face.

'Good morning,' she said with Pollyanna brightness.

'Morning.'

'How did you sleep?'

'Fine.'

She waited a beat but he still didn't turn around to greet her. 'Is something wrong?'

'No.'

Kat rolled her eyes. 'So why are you giving me the cold shoulder?'

He turned but in doing so he lost hold of one of his crutches. It clattered noisily to the floor, terrifying Cricket in the process. The poor little mutt went careening out of the room as if someone had taken a baseball bat to him. Flynn swore and tried to pick up his crutch but Kat got there first. 'Here you go,' she said.

'Thanks.' It was little more than a brooding mutter.

'Clearly someone got out of the wrong side of the bed. Am I supposed to play twenty questions or will you tell me?'

'Why didn't you stay last night?'

'I'm being paid to house-sit next door,' Kat said. 'That means I'm meant to actually house-sit. Pardon me for being a little pedantic about these things but accepting money from someone without doing the work is not something I'm all that comfortable doing.'

His tight frown relaxed slightly but didn't completely disappear. 'I'm sorry. I'm being unreasonable. Of course you have responsibilities next door.'

Kat put her hand on his forearm where he was leaning on his crutch. 'I was worried I was disturbing you last night. You were tossing and turning so much I thought your foot would get hurt if I stayed.'

There was a flicker of wryness in his smile. 'You don't take up that much space.'

'I'd better check on Cricket,' Kat said. 'Is he usually so jumpy around fallen objects?'

'My father threw a shoe at him at Christmas. I got the feeling it wasn't the first time.'

'I don't think I like either of your parents very much,' she said. 'I hope I don't have to meet them. I'm not one for keeping my opinions to myself.'

His smile set off a twinkle in his dark eyes. 'So I've found out.'

Kat reached up and planted a kiss to his mouth

before she could stop herself. 'Good morning,' she said softly.

'Good morning,' he said with equal softness. 'Do you want some breakfast? I've made coffee.'

She gave him a look of mock reproach. 'Coffee is not breakfast. You need proper nutrition when your body is repairing itself.'

He tugged on a tendril of her hair. 'Yes, dear.'

Kat laughed off his hen-pecked husband imitation. 'As if you'd ever allow a woman to tell you what you could and couldn't do. Or a man, for that matter.'

He didn't answer when she turned to go and search for Cricket, but when she glanced at him as she got to the door he was no longer smiling and that brooding frown had settled back between his brows.

The next two weeks flew past with Kat juggling rehearsals and shifts at the café. She spent most evenings with Flynn but insisted on returning to her own bed next door. The Carstairs family was coming back the following week and she wanted to make sure everything was in tip-top shape for their arrival.

On set, Elisabetta was her usual demanding self, but Kat came to look forward to their scenes together onstage. She felt inspired by the older woman's talent and knew when Elisabetta pulled her up for something it was because she knew Kat could give more, could dig deeper, could perform from her heart and soul instead of simply acting out a role. Elisabetta loved acting the way Kat loved it. It was a driving passion, an ambition she'd had since she was young.

Kat found it a little weird to have struck up a tentative friendship with her biological father's wife, but over the course of the rehearsals she felt a bond growing between Elisabetta and herself that she never would have predicted. She wouldn't have described them as friends, by any measure of the word, but she liked to think Elisabetta respected her for her willingness to learn. In a rare moment in the dressing room, Elisabetta even told Kat some of her anguish over finding out about Richard's affair with Kat's mother.

'I hated her and I hated him,' Elisabetta said,

leaning forward to apply a fresh coat of lipstick. She pressed her lips together. 'The worst thing was, he was still seeing her when he'd reconciled with me.'

'I know,' Kat said. 'I don't know how you could stay married to him after that. I would've divorced him in a flash.'

Elisabetta turned on her chair in front of the lighted mirror, her expression a little wistful. 'Have you ever been passionately in love?'

Kat opened and closed her suddenly dry mouth. 'I…erm…'

'I loved Richard from the moment I met him,' Elisabetta said. 'I looked into his eyes and wham. That was it. But I hate him too. Some days the hate wins, other days the love does. Right now, I'm undecided.'

'Do you think he's learned his lesson?' Kat asked.

Elisabetta sighed as she picked up her hairbrush. She examined it for a moment before absently drawing a couple of hairs free from the bristles. 'Who knows? Some men never do.'

Kat let a little silence pass before she asked,

'Do you think I should go to his party on Saturday? I mean, would it upset you if I did?'

Elisabetta's hand tightened on the hairbrush, the tendons on her hand standing out like white cords. But then she relaxed her hand and began brushing her hair as casually as you pleased. Swish... Swish... Swish... 'It's no skin off my nose what you do. I don't care either way.'

If Kat hadn't been an actor herself she would have believed Elisabetta. She would have taken her answer at face value. But something about the older woman's indifferent tone rang an alarm bell. What if by going to the party Kat upset Elisabetta? What could be worse at your husband's Sixty Years in Showbiz party than his dirty little secret showing up? Her friendship with Elisabetta—if you could call it that—was too fragile, too new, to compromise it. Her career was balanced on the high wire of Elisabetta's approval. She couldn't risk it. Not for the man who hadn't wanted her to be born in the first place.

*But what about Flynn?*

*He'll understand.*

*You think?*

Kat didn't want to think about it. The topic of Richard's party was the elephant in the room whenever she was with Flynn. An elephant with halitosis. Neither of them had mentioned Richard's party in the last couple of weeks. But as she walked Cricket later that day she knew she would have to give Flynn an answer one way or the other.

Flynn listened as his male client ranted about his soon-to-be-ex-wife in between raving about his replacement of her with a woman half his age. This was his fourth client today, all of them desperate to extricate themselves out of their marriages, and yet, strangely, Flynn could think of nothing but the good side of marriage. When he heard his client try and justify his actions in taking a mistress, because his wife had been sick during her pregnancy for a couple of months and not interested in sex, Flynn's back came up. What about the promise of 'in sickness and in health'? Wasn't that supposed to mean something?

He thought of Kat coming day in and day out to help him. Sure, he'd playfully blackmailed her, but she could have easily told him where to go. But instead, she had adjusted her timetable to see to his and Cricket's needs.

*His needs...*

His needs were not just physical. He could have those met in the way he used to—with a casual date for a week or two. His needs now were more cerebral. He looked forward to seeing Kat, talking to her, listening to her. Watching her. Loving her.

*Loving her.*

For once, Flynn didn't push the thought aside. He didn't shove it back behind the locked door in his brain. He didn't fight it. He let it flow through his mind, sweeping away the doubts that had lingered for too long. Of course he loved her. Hadn't he fallen in love with her that first day? Her feisty little stand-off had made him fall like a pebble kicked off a cliff. Kissing her had sealed the deal. Making love with her had cemented it. Now there was one last step he had to take to set it in stone.

To set it in stone for ever.

'Till death do us part' was a promise Flynn wanted to make. Ached to make. He had shied away from it all those years because he hadn't met the right person. The person he felt he could live with for the rest of his life. Before now, the promises had seemed claustrophobic, strangling, suffocating.

Now they made sense.

With Kat *everything* made sense.

Flynn was home by the time Kat got back from her walk with the dog. He was in the sitting room but instead of sitting on the sofa with his foot up he was standing on his crutches looking out of the window. He turned when she came in but his expression was difficult to read. 'Hi.'

'Hi.'

Was he going to come over and kiss her like he usually did? Why was he standing all the way over there? He didn't even seem aware of Cricket, who was dancing around his ankles in a frenzy of delight. But then, as if the little dog sensed the gravity of Flynn's mood, he lowered himself to the floor in a submissive 'stay' position, his scruffy little head resting on his paws.

'Is…is something wrong?' Kat asked. 'You

seem a little tense. Not just today but for the last couple of weeks. Is it work? Your foot? Your family?' *Me?*

He gave her a smile that only involved half his mouth. 'I've been waiting for you.'

Kat hung up her coat, pulled off her gloves and put them on the hallstand. 'I told you I was going to be late. We had to do a dress rehearsal and then Elisabetta had an issue with the way her hair was done. Honestly, she can be such a pain in the butt.'

There was a weird little silence.

She looked at him again, her heart jerking as if it had been kicked. 'Why are you looking at me like that?'

His expression lost its surface tension, as if something deep inside him had softened. Melted. 'I never thought I'd do this again.'

'Do what?'

'Ask someone to marry me.'

Kat stared at him in a stunned silence. She blinked and opened her mouth to speak but no words came out. Shock ran through her like a stupefying drug. She couldn't get her thoughts to process properly. It was as though someone had scrambled her brain, shaken it up until none of her synapses were connecting. Why would he ask her to marry him? He wasn't in love with her...was he? He had never said. Never hinted. Not one word.

Flynn came closer and, leaning on one crutch, cupped her cheek in his hand. 'I'm sorry I can't get down on bended knee but I love you, Kat. I want you to marry me. Please will you do me the honour of becoming my wife?'

*He's only asking you because of the party.*

*No, he's not. He said he loves me.*

*Yeah, right. The party is on Saturday. This is his insurance policy.*

Kat felt like she was balanced over a canyon on a toothpick. How could she know for sure what his motives were? He had set his mind on getting her to that party. She would not be able to say no if she was officially engaged to him. It would look odd if she didn't show. He was Richard's legal advisor, a part of the family—a close friend to all the Ravensdales. 'This seems rather...sudden...'

His mouth did that rueful half-twist again. 'I know, but once I make my mind up about something I have to act. Let's not waste any more time pretending we don't care for each other. We belong together, darling. We both felt it the first time we met.'

*Don't do it.*

*But I want to say yes!*

*You need more time. What about your career? 'Fools rush in' and all that.*

The tender look on Flynn's face overrode her doubts. 'You love me?'

His smile made her heart squeeze as tightly as a child's hug. 'How can you doubt it?'

Kat stepped up to him and wrapped her arms around his waist, looking up at his adoring expression. How could this be happening? It was so much more than she'd expected. She hadn't dared expect anything. She had tried to keep her heart out of reach but it had been impossible. Resisting Flynn Carlyon had been impossible. Stopping herself from falling in love with him had been impossible. 'But I thought you were against marriage?'

He cradled her face in one of his large hands. 'Not when it involves you. I can't think of anyone else I would want to spend the rest of my life bantering with. Can you?'

Kat smiled. 'No.'

His black-coffee eyes twinkled. 'So, is that a yes?'

She brought her mouth up to meet his descending one. 'Yes. A thousand, million, squillion times yes.'

The kiss was getting a little more serious when Kat became aware of Flynn's phone ringing. He had different tones for different people but she had never heard this ring tone before. She eased back to look up at him. 'Are you going to answer it?'

'It's not important. It's just Richard.'

A cold handprint touched the back of her neck. 'Why's he calling you now?'

'He calls me most days.'

Kat searched his expression...for what, she wasn't sure. Something didn't feel right. She couldn't explain it. It had been fine until that phone had started ringing. She couldn't help feeling it was like the sounding of an alarm bell. She could see the rectangular outline of his phone inside his shirt pocket.

She heard it ping with a left message.

She reached for it at the same time Flynn did, his hand stilling hers. Warning hers.

'I want to see that message,' she said.

'No.'

Kat raised her brow at his intractable tone. 'Why not?'

'It's private.'

'But I'm your fiancée. You get to share everything with me.'

Something hardened in his jaw. A muscle. A ligament. It travelled all the way to his mouth. 'Not about my clients.'

'He's my father, so surely that's different?'

'It's not.'

Kat knew he was right to insist on client confidentiality but she couldn't get rid of the cloud of doubt blurring her vision of the future. Their future. 'So does that mean you won't allow me access to your phone once we're married?'

The tension around his mouth tightened. 'Trust is a huge part of being married.'

'Does that mean I get to keep my phone and emails private too?'

She could see the battle played out on his face. It was like a tug of war between logic and emotion. Push. Pull. Push. Pull. 'If you insist.'

'I do.'

The phone rang again. Same tone. Same insistent clarion call. Flynn took it out of his pocket and, giving Kat an unreadable look, answered it. 'Richard, I'm busy right now. I'll call you ba—'

'Did you get her to agree to come to the party?' Richard's voice carried like a foghorn.

Kat's spine went rigid. Ice-block rigid. Don't-mess-with-me-rigid. She held out her hand for the phone. 'I want to speak to him.'

Flynn held the phone against his chest. 'I don't think that's such a great idea.'

She kept her hand out, her eyes locked on his, her determination on fire. 'Give me the damn phone.'

'Is that Kat I can hear in the background?' The

fabric of Flynn's shirt only faintly muffled Richard's theatre-trained voice. 'Let me talk to her.'

Flynn handed her the phone with a look that suggested he felt like he was handing over a live bomb.

'This is Kat Winwood.'

'Kat, my dear.' Richard's voice was all treacle, honey and sickly-sweet jam. 'How lovely to hear your voice at last. Are you coming to the party? Did Flynn make it impossible for you to refuse, as I instructed him?'

Kat's hand tightened on the phone. She wanted to throw it at the wall. To smash it on the floor. To stomp on it until the screen shattered, like her dream had been shattered. 'No,' she said, casting Flynn a look that said, *This includes you.* 'I've decided not to come to the party and my decision is final.'

'But my sweet child,' Richard said, 'it won't be the same without you there.'

'You'll get over it,' Kat said and handed the phone back to Flynn.

Flynn clicked off the call and put the phone back in his pocket without saying anything to

Richard. 'Come on, Kat. You surely don't think I staged my proposal to get you to—?'

'Why ask me today? Why not ask me after the weekend when the party is over?'

A muscle worked like a hammer in his jaw. Tap. Tap. Tap. 'How can you possibly *think* that? Haven't the last few weeks shown you how much I care about you? What does it matter when I ask you? The important thing is that I ask you. I love you. Why would I wait?'

Kat reached for her coat, shoving her arms through the sleeves so roughly the lining tore. How could she trust he was being genuine? She was torn; she wanted to believe he loved her but what if it was all a ruse to get her to meet her father in person? Flynn didn't like losing. He had set himself a goal and he let nothing and no one get in his way of achieving it. There was a streak of ruthlessness in him. She had seen that from the first time she'd met him.

But would he really go so far as to *propose* to her to achieve his mission?

'I'm not going to ask you again,' Flynn said in a hard, tight voice. 'Take it or leave it.'

Kat turned to look at him with an implacable set to her features. 'You should know me well enough by now to know I don't tolerate ultimatums.'

His frown turned his eyebrows into a single intimidating line. 'I'll make arrangements for someone else to walk Cricket. You're relieved from your responsibilities here as of now.'

Kat kept her spine straight, her shoulders aligned, her resolve rimmed with steel. 'You're acting like a child who's thrown its favourite toy out of the sandpit.'

He gave a rough laugh. '*I'm* acting like a child? What about you? You won't admit to your feelings about me because you're frightened of allowing someone close in case they let you down.'

'I'm not in love with you.' Kat used every ounce of acting ability she possessed. 'I'm in love with my career. That's all I want for now. It's all I've ever wanted.'

His top lip curled, his dark eyes flashed. 'I hope it keeps you warm at night because, after all the lights are down and the adoring fans have all gone home, you'll be on your own.'

# CHAPTER TWELVE

FLYNN COULDN'T WAIT for the party to be over. It was a slow, miserable torture watching the Ravensdale siblings with their partners. It was a painful reminder of what he had lost. No one was looking at him with love shining in their eyes. He had no one he could slip his arm around and draw close. No one to exchange a look with that spoke of love, hope, the future.

He was alone.

Miranda approached with a plate of nibbles. 'Shame about Kat not coming.'

'Yeah, well, can't say I didn't try.'

'Maybe she just needs more time.'

'How much time?' Flynn couldn't keep the frustration out of his tone. 'When you know, you just know, right?'

Miranda's eyes rounded. 'You asked her to *marry* you?'

He swiped a hand down his face as if to swipe away the memory of his failure. How could he have got it so wrong? 'Maybe I need proposal lessons or something.'

'It's probably not your proposal that's the issue,' Miranda said. 'It's your timing.'

Flynn looked down at her heart-shaped face with those big Bambi eyes brimming with concern. Had he mistimed it? Would he get a different answer if he asked again? 'Maybe. Maybe not.' *Maybe I'm destined to be alone.*

'Dad's party was always going to be an issue for her,' Miranda said. 'She saw it as your mission. She probably couldn't separate it from her feelings for you.'

Hope flicked a match inside his chest, the warmth spreading as it took hold. 'You reckon she has feelings for me?'

Miranda gave him a 'get real' look. 'You men can be so blind at times. Of course she loves you. All the signs are there.'

'She hasn't said anything…I mean, she never actually said the words.'

'In the best relationships you don't need to.'

As if to confirm it, Leandro looked at Miranda from across the room where he was standing next to Richard. His look said it all: 'I love you and I can't wait for this evening to be over so we can be alone'.

Miranda's cheeks blushed a dusky rose. 'I'd better rescue him. That's the third soliloquy he's suffered tonight about Dad's brilliance.'

Flynn's chest cramped when he saw Leandro's arm slip around Miranda's waist and draw her close. Flynn shifted his gaze and saw Julius and Holly, and his heart squeezed again. Harder. Like a vice squashing an over-ripe peach. One of the waiters passed with a tray of drinks and Holly shook her head, one of her hands going protectively over her abdomen. The look Julius gave her was so proud, so full of love, it made Flynn feel all the more achingly alone.

Jaz appeared by his side with her usual impishness. 'Why the long face?'

He sent her a look that told her to back off. 'Where's Jake? Chatting up one of the waitresses?'

She laughed a tinkling-bell laugh. 'No, he's still

recovering from meeting me in the cloakroom. Here he comes now.'

Jake strutted into the room, straightening his tie, his eyes meeting Jaz's with a satisfied gleam. He pulled Jaz to his side. 'Find your own girl. This one's mine.'

Flynn gave him a rictus smile. A been-dead-for-a- month rictus smile. 'I'm working on it.'

Jake swept his gaze around the room. 'No Kat?'

'Nope.'

'Pity.'

'Yeah.'

The silence stretched.

'You're really serious about her.' Jake didn't say it as a question, more of a statement. An observation of truth.

'Yes. I am.'

'You going to ask the big question?'

'I already have.'

Jake's dark brows shot up. 'You did?'

'Yep. She said no.'

Jake's chin went back against his neck in disgust. 'You asked her *before* the party? Are you out of your freaking mind?'

He was out of his mind. Out of his mind with love. Out of his mind with impatience for this wretched party to be over so he could go to Kat and sort this out. 'I know, I know, I know. Bad timing.'

'You could skip the speeches and head back to London,' Jack said.

'I made a promise to your father.'

'Yeah, well, does it look like he's disappointed his love child didn't show?' Jake's tone was cynicism on steroids. 'At least Mum's here.'

Flynn looked across to where Elisabetta was working the floor like the superstar she was. She was never happier than when she was centre-stage. Even though she'd threatened not to turn up, she couldn't help herself. Any chance to take the spotlight off Richard and shine it on her instead was too tempting.

A thought took hold. What if Kat couldn't stop herself from attending? What if she had changed her mind? What if her desire to meet her half-brothers had overridden her desire to distance herself from her father?

Flynn swept his gaze over the crowded room.

There was no sign of her. But for the last few minutes the back of his neck had prickled, like radar picking up a faint signal.

But then he heard something… Cricket was barking outside on the terrace with the smokers, where he had ordered him to stay. Barking madly. Joyfully.

Flynn smiled. He knew what that bark was.

It was a bark of recognition.

Kat had decided to gatecrash the party but not as herself. She wanted to see her family without them seeing her. She wanted to see Flynn too. To see if he had moved on in the two days since she had rejected his proposal. Would he be flirting with one of the beautiful people at the party? Or would he be feeling like she did? Miserable and empty, as if someone had scraped out her heart and her belly?

But she hadn't factored in Cricket.

Her disguise had fooled the paparazzi hanging around the entrance to Ravensdene. It had fooled the catering staff manager when she'd signed on for duty in the kitchen. She hadn't tested it on

Flynn because she had been assigned the back half of the house for the first half of her shift. But she was no match for Cricket. As soon as she came outside with a tray of drinks for the smokers on the terrace, he recognised her. He danced around her ankles, spinning and leaping and panting in excitement. She put the tray she was carrying on a table and bent down to him. 'Hush. Don't blow my cover. I'm not meant to be here.'

*Then why are you?*

*Because I might have been a bit hasty in my judgment.*

*You've blown it. He said he was only going to ask you once.*

*I know, but I need to see him. Just the once. Just in case I've got it wrong.*

Kat straightened once Cricket had settled down. Well, marginally, that was. He kept following her like a devoted slave, his tongue hanging out, his little beady eyes dancing as if he knew he was in on her secret.

Kat was about to go back inside when Flynn

came out on the terrace. 'Cricket, leave the wait-ress alone.'

*The waitress?*

*Of course he won't recognise me. I'm blonde tonight, with glasses. And heaps of make-up.*

*If he were truly in love with you, he'd recog-nise you anywhere in any disguise.*

Flynn leaned against the balustrade on the ter-race, resting his crutches beside him. 'Could you bring me a drink?'

Kat approached him warily. 'Orange juice is all I have left.' She was quite proud of her English accent. Maybe she wouldn't need a voice coach after all.

He took the glass and, without looking at her, knocked half of it back. 'Thanks.'

Kat knew she should have moved on but it an-noyed her that he hadn't recognised her. Really annoyed her, which was ridiculously inconsistent of her. But still. 'Will that be all?'

'Yep.' He knocked back the rest of his drink and handed her the glass, again without looking at her.

She waited a beat. 'Would you like me to bring you some food? A plate of nibbles?'

'No thanks.'

'Another drink?'

'Not in the mood for celebrating.'

'Oh?'

He let out a long-drawn-out breath. 'It's a long story. I won't bore you with it when you've got work to do.'

'I'm not busy.' Kat mentally kicked herself. 'I mean…I've got a minute or two…'

He gave her a brief glance, the sort of glance you gave catering staff that you expect never to see again. 'Ever been in love?'

Kat looked down at Cricket who was looking up at her with that black-button gaze. 'I have, actually.'

'It sucks.'

She glanced back at Flynn. He was studying his bandaged foot with a frown so deep it had joined his eyebrows. 'Why do you think it sucks?' she said.

'If the person you love doesn't love you back, then it sucks. Big-time.'

'How do you know she doesn't love you back?'

'She never said the words.'

'But that doesn't mean she doesn't love you,' Kat said. 'It just means she was a little uncertain of the circumstances under which you proposed.'

He looked at her then in puzzlement. 'How do you know I proposed?'

Kat gave a short, uncertain laugh. 'Flynn…it's me. It's Kat. Don't you recognise me?'

A smile began in his eyes well before it appeared on his mouth. 'Of course I recognise you, you little goose. You love me? Really?'

Happiness burst inside Kat's chest like a flower exploding. 'I do.'

'That's twice you've said "I do" to me. Do you reckon you could say it one more time in front of a minister of religion so I can get a ring on your finger?'

Kat was torn between wanting to punch his arm for messing with her head and throwing her arms around him and kissing him. Kissing him won. She threw her arms around him, almost knocking him backwards off the terrace. 'You want to get married in church?'

'Anywhere that makes it official.'

She couldn't wipe the smile off her face. 'I'm sorry for rejecting you the first time. I just had to make sure you really loved me.'

He brushed a strand of blonde wig back behind her ear. 'I didn't think it was possible to love someone as much as I love you. Life loses all its colour without you in it.'

Kat stroked his face. 'These last couple of days have been torture. I've been so lonely and miserable. I couldn't bear another minute without seeing you.'

'How did you land the waitress job without alerting Richard's security team?'

She gave him a sheepish look. 'Well, I had to tell someone, otherwise I would never have got in. He said he would keep it a secret but I didn't factor in Cricket.'

'Yeah, well, I still haven't figured out boarding arrangements for him,' Flynn said. 'I knew as soon as I heard him barking that you were here.'

'Do you think you would've recognised me anyway?'

He touched her nose with his fingertip. 'Sure of it. My body picks you up like radar.'

Kat grinned. 'Mine too.'

Flynn took her hand and held it against his chest. 'Time to meet the family...or would you like to stay incognito?'

Kat pulled at her lip with her teeth. 'Do you think it would annoy Elisabetta? I don't want to upset her. I have to get through a season with her, remember.'

'You could stay disguised, but I'm going to have a heck of time explaining to your brothers why I've been kissing the blonde waitress.' Flynn gave a rueful grimace. 'Too late. Here they come now.'

Kat turned to see her twin half-brothers come out of the French doors. It was a surreal moment to meet them in the flesh. They were exactly alike, especially when they both smiled once they realised what was going on.

'Welcome to the family,' Julius said. 'I hope you know what you're letting yourself in for.'

'I think I'll cope,' Kat said.

Jake gave her a brotherly hug. 'Welcome to Mayhem Manor.'

Miranda and Jaz came out with Holly close behind. There were lots of hugs and words of welcome. The warmth of her family made Kat's heart swell so much, she had difficulty drawing breath.

*Her family.*

But then another person walked out to the terrace.

Her father.

Kat took a deep breath as he came towards her. She wasn't sure what she was supposed to feel. She didn't love him. She didn't even like him. But for the sake of appearances and the rest of the family she held out her hand to him. 'Hello.'

Richard ignored her hand and hugged her, just long enough for the cameras to document it. 'Welcome to the family, my dear.'

Elisabetta sauntered out with a glass of champagne in one hand, her expression one of acute boredom, although Kat was sure she could detect a hint of secretive delight in that dark-brown gaze. 'So, you've sorted it all out, Flynn?'

'Not quite.'

Kat glanced at Flynn who had hopped on his crutches to where she was standing surrounded by her family. 'What else needs to be sorted?' she said.

'You haven't said you love me. I'm not going back inside the house until you do.'

Kat gave him a teasing smile. 'Is that an ultimatum?'

His answering smile made the backs of her knees tingle. 'Something I should warn you about before we marry—I *always* win.'

Kat took him by the tie and pulled his head down. 'Guess what? So do I.'

\* \* \* \* \*

# MILLS & BOON®
## Large Print – September 2016

**Morelli's Mistress**
Anne Mather

**A Tycoon to Be Reckoned With**
Julia James

**Billionaire Without a Past**
Carol Marinelli

**The Shock Cassano Baby**
Andie Brock

**The Most Scandalous Ravensdale**
Melanie Milburne

**The Sheikh's Last Mistress**
Rachael Thomas

**Claiming the Royal Innocent**
Jennifer Hayward

**The Billionaire Who Saw Her Beauty**
Rebecca Winters

**In the Boss's Castle**
Jessica Gilmore

**One Week with the French Tycoon**
Christy McKellen

**Rafael's Contract Bride**
Nina Milne

# MILLS & BOON®
## Large Print – October 2016

**Wallflower, Widow...Wife!**
Ann Lethbridge

**Bought for the Greek's Revenge**
Lynne Graham

**An Heir to Make a Marriage**
Abby Green

**The Greek's Nine-Month Redemption**
Maisey Yates

**Expecting a Royal Scandal**
Caitlin Crews

**Return of the Untamed Billionaire**
Carol Marinelli

**Signed Over to Santino**
Maya Blake

**Wedded, Bedded, Betrayed**
Michelle Smart

**The Greek's Nine-Month Surprise**
Jennifer Faye

**A Baby to Save Their Marriage**
Scarlet Wilson

**Stranded with Her Rescuer**
Nikki Logan

**Expecting the Fellani Heir**
Lucy Gordon

0916 Rom LP